Fingers laced the length of her hair

"Your hair is like sunshine," Adam said huskily as he lifted a strand to his lips.

Jess caught her breath as he loosened her blouse until her lacy bra was exposed. Waves of sensation threatened to drown her. His touch was bringing every nerve to stinging life.

Adam smiled, but his eyes followed his fingers, touching lightly as they traveled the border of lace and outlined the full curve of her breast. They seemed to have a life of their own as they slipped inside the lacy cup. She gasped as they sought and discovered a hardening nipple. "Please, no!" she choked.

He lowered his lips to a tiny mole.

Jessica felt her will drain away, and abandoned herself to the fire he had ignited.

WELCOME
TO THE WONDERFUL WORLD
OF *Harlequin Romances*

The Beachcomber

Marion Smith

Harlequin Books

TORONTO • NEW YORK • LONDON
AMSTERDAM • PARIS • SYDNEY • HAMBURG
STOCKHOLM • ATHENS • TOKYO • MILAN

Original hardcover edition published in 1983
by Mills & Boon Limited

ISBN 0-373-02598-X

Harlequin Romance first edition January 1984

Printed in U.S.A.

CHAPTER ONE

THE forlorn figure of a slight girl wandered aimlessly along the white sandy beach. There were faint tracks behind her for as far as the eye could see; sometimes flirting with the foam-edged water, sometimes climbing the slight rise of the dunes to meander through graceful plumes of sawgrass. The sky had darkened, but Jessica Gentry was oblivious to the crashing surf and the billowing thunderclouds overhead. She was immersed in her own thoughts, worried lines marring her brow. She kicked at the sand with the toe of her sneaker in frustration, and took a shuddering breath to swallow the tears that burned behind her eyes.

'Hey, Beachcomber!' A deep voice penetrated the haze surrounding her.

Jessica raised bewildered eyes to the steely grey ones of the man standing a few feet away. She was so absorbed that his startling good looks barely registered at first. But, as his gaze locked with hers, she felt a kindling spark ignite within her. There was a warm tingling at the back of her neck, which descended slowly down her spine and circled her body like a pair of comforting arms. Her heart lifted, then settled back to pound rhythmically in her breast as she stared at the man.

He too seemed unable to tear his eyes away. Their colour softened, then darkened. An exceptional strength and vitality reached out to her from his broad-shouldered frame. The hollow in his rugged cheek deepened.

As she looked at him Jessica had the most extraordinary sensation that some sort of unspoken message had passed between them. Even the deserted beach faded as they looked at each other in wonder.

How long they stood there she didn't know, but when he murmured her name softly, she wasn't surprised. It was as natural as the tides, that he knew her; just as she knew him.

She had never seen this man before, but his features were familiar; in a dream she had explored them with the tips of her fingers. She had traced the heavy brows, outlined the sensual masculine mouth. A momentary cloud of puzzlement dimmed her eyes, and he answered, though she hadn't asked, 'Adam.'

'Adam,' she breathed softly. His gaze dropped to her lips when she said his name, and the kiss in his eyes was real. She felt his mouth on hers, although he hadn't moved.

Suddenly a distant clap of thunder intruded, breaking the spell and bringing a frown to his face. He took a breath and raised his head. His eyes swept the sky. 'There's a storm brewing.

You'd better get home.'

Jessica wondered vaguely why he seemed to withdraw. His voice was harsh, almost angry.

Lifting her face to the dark clouds, she winced when a large raindrop fell on her cheek. 'You're right—I'd better hurry. Goodbye,' she murmured, a question in her eyes.

'Goodbye, Jessica.' His tone was final.

Reluctantly, she turned to retrace her steps. She had covered only a short distance when, unable to resist, she looked back over her shoulder at him.

The man Adam, who still watched her, was probably in his early thirties. He was a big man, well over six feet tall, and his khaki pants were moulded to muscular thighs. A navy blue windbreaker was casually zipped over a powerful chest and broad shoulders. He turned the collar up against the rain and it brushed his dark, springy hair.

Raising his hand in an easy salute, Adam started to walk slowly towards a rock and glass house, just visible behind the dunes. His brows knitted in a frown when he paused to look back at the girl moving away from him. Without warning a bolt of lightning pierced the sky, and the smell of sulphur was strong in his nostrils. He did an about-face at the top of the dunes, shouting to Jessica. The wind had quickened. It carried his voice back to him when he called to her again.

Jessica kept walking, as if in a trance. She

hardly noticed that the drops were becoming a deluge and the lightning was dangerously near, until Adam scooped her up into his arms as easily as a kitten. Surprised by his sudden action, she clutched at him, her hands circling his neck.

Holding her close to his broad chest, Adam crossed the dunes with long strides and mounted steps to a covered deck which ran the length of the house. Even with his haste they were both soaked.

'You little idiot!' he snapped, setting her on her feet. His strong hands grasped her shoulders and he gave her an impatient shake.

Jessica was overwhelmingly aware of his strength, but not alarmed. She looked up into his stern face, her expression trusting.

Adam caught his breath. His hands tightened for a moment and he seemed to search for something far down in the violet blue of her eyes. Then slowly he smiled. The smile transformed his face, softening the craggy features, and holding her spellbound. His hands dropped reluctantly from her shoulders and his voice was gentler as he apologised, 'I'm sorry I snapped.'

With dawning awareness of his attraction, Jessica smiled, too. Her face was lit from within. The glow brought a slight flush to her cheeks, deepened the colour of her eyes.

Adam started to reach for her again, but then with an effort, he tore his gaze away. He turned to open one of the sliding glass doors which made up the entire wall of the house facing the ocean. 'You'd better come inside until the storm passes over.' He grinned wryly. 'The Golden Isles of Georgia aren't so golden today. January isn't the ideal time for beachcombing.'

Jessica blushed as she looked down at what she was wearing; an old, very faded pair of jeans, her favourite sneakers with a strategic hole in the toe, and a cast-off sweat-shirt of her brother's. Her long blonde hair was in a single braid down her back. I suppose I do look a bit like a beachcomber, she thought. Mother would say 'I told you so!' At the thought of her mother's reaction to her appearance a dimple played briefly in her cheek.

All at once she was herself again. She seemed to wake from a confusing dream, and her smile widened in genuine amusement. 'Thank you,' she replied. 'If you don't mind, I would like to call someone to pick me up.'

As she stepped through the open door an ear-splitting crash of thunder reverberated around them, and a small scream escaped her lips. She turned instinctively into Adam's waiting arms and they tightened possessively around her. Her face was burrowed in his chest and he cradled her head in his big hand for a moment. She could feel his heart racing against her cheek.

Adam sighed. His hand moved down her back in a firm caress before he dropped his arms.

Taking a step away from her, he shoved his hands into his pockets.

Jessica was embarrassed and color flooded her face as she moved further into the room. 'I'm sorry—I don't usually throw myself at perfect strangers. The thunder startled me,' she explained, her voice shaking slightly.

'You know better than that, Jessica,' he said tightly. He led her to a fireplace where flames burned cheerfully. 'Sit there on the hearth. I'll be right back.'

'Better than what?' She sat down on the rock ledge, grateful for the warmth of the fire. She didn't look at him when she asked the question.

Adam came down on his haunches beside her, and tilted her chin with a finger. She couldn't avoid his eyes, and again she was back in that confusing dream.

'I'm not a stranger,' he said huskily.

Before she could recover he had left the room through a swinging door at the other end. Jolted by the raw maleness of him, she shivered in her wet clothes and edged closer to the fire. A bit late, she asked herself, how did he know her name? Who was he?

Her father had only recently retired from the practice of law, and they had moved from Washington, D.C. to this beautiful coastal area. This handsome stranger was not a part of the lively, party-loving group of young people she had met. He was definitely not a man you would forget soon. If ever, Jessica added mentally.

Sighing, she looked around her at the starkly dramatic room. White walls and vaulted ceiling were divided by heavy dark wooden beams. Opposite the wall of glass, the rock fireplace where she sat soared to the roof two stories high. Large stuffed armchairs and a sofa were upholstered in supple glowing leather the colour of polished mahogany. At right angles to the fireplace was a businesslike desk, cluttered with books, papers, and empty coffee cups. A typewriter was bathed in light from a chrome and brass lamp. Evidence of frustration was in the white balls of paper littering the floor around an overflowing trash can.

Adam returned to the room carrying two brandy snifters. 'Get this inside you to ward off the chill. I've started some coffee.'

'Thank you,' she said, accepting the globe of glass. 'You have the advantage of me, Mr——' She paused, waiting for him to fill in the name.

His eyes met and held hers and once more she couldn't look away. What on earth was wrong with her? She felt her heartbeat accelerate. He only had to look at her and she was almost paralysed. No man had ever had this effect on her before. All movement seemed to be in slow motion. Forcing her eyes down to the brandy glass, she lifted it to sip.

'My name is Adam Oakman.' He searched her

face for a reaction before continuing, 'I'm a friend of your brother Dennis.' He chuckled. 'I'll have to admit that it took me a minute to recognise you from the picture of the sophisticated young lady in the leather folder Dennis carries around with him!'

A gleam of hope flared in her eyes at the mention of her brother, only to be replaced swiftly by wariness. Carefully she set the glass down. 'You know Dennis?' she asked slowly.

'Very well.'

Her beloved brother—where was he? The fears that had flooded her mind as she walked on the beach returned, and she twisted her head to hide the tears that threatened. Dennis had warned her that he might not be heard from for a while and not to discuss his absence with anyone. He had been adamant about that, but three weeks had passed without a word from him. Jessica couldn't rid herself of the feeling that he was in terrible danger. She longed to question Adam Oakman, but Dennis had said emphatically, 'No one!' So instead she stood and moved to the telephone on the desk, saying brightly, 'Well, well, small world, as they say. I'd better call a taxi to come and pick me up. Do you have a telephone directory?'

Adam frowned at the flippancy in her tone. He watched the delicate profile as her eyes scanned the desk, looking for the book. His expression gave nothing away when he spoke. 'There's no need for that. I'll run you home shortly. I'm expecting a call, but while we're waiting we can have a shower and I'll dry your clothes.'

Her back stiffened. She thought warily, what have I got myself into? I'm certainly not going to take a shower in a strange man's house!

Aloud she said, 'No, thank you. The fire will dry me out nicely.' Moving back to the raised hearth, she stretched long fingers towards the warmth of the blaze. Despite herself she sneezed. 'Some coffee would be good, though. Did you say you were making some?'

Adam laughed. 'Now, Jessica, what would Dennis think of me if I let his little sister come down with pneumonia?' He spoke to her rigid back.

'Dennis isn't here,' she said stiffly.

'Would you feel more inclined if Dennis vouched for me?' he asked quietly.

She hesitated, then nodded.

His hands turned her to face him. She felt the warmth of their touch on her arms even through the heavy fabric of the sweat-shirt. There was a determined line to his jaw as he looked down at her.

Jessica resisted his magnetic attraction. This was a potentially dangerous situation. She shouldn't be in this house, and, even though she still felt no alarm; her common sense belatedly began to assert itself.

Suddenly Adam grasped her arm and propelled

her ahead of him, across the room and through an arch into a hallway. Panicked, she tried to pull away, but he continued down the hall to the open door of a bedroom.

'No!' She whirled to face him, but he had moved to a closet door. 'I don't want a shower.'

'Yes, Jessica!' Then he grinned. 'The call I'm expecting is from Dennis,' he said. Ignoring her shocked gasp, he went on, 'You can ask him about me then. In the meantime, here's a robe.' He tossed something soft into her arms. 'The bathroom's through that door. There's a hair dryer in the top dresser drawer. Use it!'

As he left the room he paused, letting his eyes roam slowly over her. They left heat wherever they touched. By the time he finished his unhurried inspection, Jessica was breathless. She clutched the robe and stared at him.

'Did you think I meant for us to shower together, Beachcomber? I must admit, now that you've given me the idea, it's an intriguing one!' He grinned, then chuckled at her expression. 'Close your mouth!'

Jessica clamped her lips shut as he left the room, then smiled wryly at herself. She had never reacted to a man like she did to this one—or perhaps overreacted was a better word. There was something about him that sent her emotions into a whirlpool of confusion.

She had always kept men at arm's length, preferring relaxed friendships to the soul-rocking love affairs her friends talked about. She never lacked dates, but avoided getting too involved. She knew that some of the men she had dated regarded her as a prude, but Dennis had always told her there was nothing wrong with being a prude. Dennis!

Adam had said that he was going to call. Why would he call here? She frowned. How good a friend was Adam? If only she could talk to someone!

Dennis, like their father, was a lawyer. After graduation from law school, he had tried a few years as a very junior partner in Dad's lucrative private practice in Washington. But the everyday practice of law didn't appeal to his sense of adventure, so he had chosen to join the Justice Department. A month ago he had been sent to this area to act as undercover head of a justice strike team.

Jessica had been delighted. Though there was a nine-year age difference, she and Dennis were close and she had missed him since she moved to Georgia with their parents.

But she hadn't realised what undercover meant. So far their only communication was by very infrequent phone calls, the last one, three weeks ago.

Dennis had told her that the strike team was investigating the prolific drug traffic, coming in across the coast, despite herculean efforts by the local authorities. So many millions of dollars were involved that the criminals would often beach a large boat, remove the drugs and abandon the craft, especially if the Coast Guard were close on their heels. Cohorts would be waiting nearby with transportation and the whole process could be completed in a very short period of time. Planes were also used in the same way, flying in low over the beach and landing in a field or on a back country road. The speed of the operation made it extremely difficult to apprehend the criminals.

Dennis had explained all this to her. The death and destruction of human life meant nothing to these people. Jessica knew that he was in danger because they would stop at nothing to protect the enormous profit involved.

And, she thought, who is Adam Oakman?

A knock on the door interrupted her turbulent thoughts. 'Give me your wet things, Jessica, and I'll toss them into the dryer.'

She hesitated. 'Ju-just a minute.' This wasn't smart, she told herself, but her clothes were soaked. She had an idea that even if she protested he would have his way.

Dropping the white terrycloth robe to the floor, she quickly stripped off her shirt and jeans. Opening the door a crack, she handed them through.

A hard hand held the door as she would have closed it. 'All of them,' said Adam firmly.

'No.' Her breath was deserting her again.

'Jessica, I don't have a lot of patience. Do you want me to come in there and get them?' he asked silkily.

'No! No, I don't want you to do that.' Quickly she unhooked her bra and stepped out of her panties. She grabbed for the robe to hold in front of her, then still hiding behind the door, she thrust them through the crack. 'There! Now will you please close this door?'

A deep chuckle reached her ears.

What now? she thought.

'Jessica, Jessica,' he sighed, 'what a mind you have! These are very enticing and I have a normal male reaction to sexy bits of lace, but I meant your sneakers. You can't go home in wet shoes!'

Her temper rose at his mocking tone. 'Well, you may have meant sneakers, but that wasn't what you implied, and you know it!' Her words were clipped, but her face was crimson as she handed him the shoes. He was laughing! She slammed the door with a decisive bang and stalked to the bathroom, muttering to herself.

The hot water felt wonderfully good cascading over her chilled body. She removed the fastener from her hair and began to unbraid it. Loosened, it fell almost to her waist. There was shampoo on the shower shelf, and when she opened the bottle and poured a few drops into her hand, the scent of a light perfume drifted up to her nostrils. She wrinkled her nose and frowned. This definitely was not Adam Oakman's. Who was the woman?

she wondered. Jessica didn't realise that her lovely lower lip made a decisive pout!

She stepped from the shower and wrapped herself in the white robe. As she rubbed her hair partially dry with a towel, she wandered back into the bedroom to look for the dryer. On the dresser was a silver-backed comb and brush, and again she felt a twinge, wondering who they belonged to. She ran the comb through the long, thick golden strands and flipped on the hand-held blow-dryer. The warm air about her head alleviated the rest of the chill, and she looked around her. This was certainly a woman's room. Soft shades of blue draped the windows and bed, and a gold velvet slipper chair reflected the colour of the plush carpet beneath her bare feet.

Was Adam married? The thought was depressing. She didn't want him to be married. The hand holding the dryer froze. Disconcerting thoughts tumbled over each other in her mind.

Suddenly . . . suddenly she knew that she couldn't bear the idea that he might be married! A powerful emotion swept through her, leaving her knees weak, and she sank down on the edge of the bed, staring, beyond the room, beyond space, into her mind, her soul. Love at first sight?

Her mind answered, Impossible! In novels, but not in real life. Infatuation? Probably. You couldn't love someone until you knew them. Could you?

But she did know him, her soul told her. She

knew nothing about him, and everything. That was why she had turned instinctively to him when the thunder had frightened her. She knew him and she loved him.

This was crazy! Jessica switched off the dryer which rested uselessly in her lap, and dropped it on the bed. She rose. Crossing the room to the window, she looked with troubled eyes across the sea. Who was this man? There were too many disturbances in her life at the present time to take anyone at face value. The name Adam Oakman meant nothing to her.

He did seem to know a lot about Dennis. The small leather folder that her brother always carried was a personal item, one that Dennis didn't show to just anyone. For him to be familiar with it was encouraging. But where had Adam come from? The meeting on the beach was almost too providential. And why was he waiting for Dennis to call him? Her brows came together across puzzled blue eyes. She gave the ties that wrapped the robe a sharp tug and picked up the dryer to replace it in the drawer.

Catching her reflection in the mirror above, she paused. She didn't look different. Or did she? She leaned closer. Surely there was a sparkle in her eyes, a glow, that hadn't been there before. She picked up the silver-backed brush and studied it soberly. The question of whose room this was hadn't been answered.

Jessica had always realised that she was not a

particularly practical person. She had come along rather late in her parents' life, when they had the leisure to be indulgent, and having a much older brother to guide her through any scrapes she got herself into, she had slipped effortlessly into adulthood. She had never been denied anything she really wanted, and her basic honesty made her admit that she was probably spoiled.

She prayed silently, 'Please don't let him be married.' If Adam were married . . . well, she would have to do some growing up in a hurry, and all on her own.

Her silken hair had finally dried into soft waves and tendrils which framed her face. She twisted it up to the top of her head and fastened it, then she tightened the sash of the robe around her and took a deep breath.

Opening the door to the hall, she stepped tentatively out of the room.

'Feeling better?'

Jessica whirled at the question from behind her.

Adam had changed into dry clothes. He wore dark brown drill pants, and the white turtleneck sweater made his tanned features even darker.

In the light of her new knowledge, Jessica's hands began to tremble at the sight of that hard masculine body. She hid them in the pockets of the robe and dropped her eyes from the penetrating stare of his grey ones.

'Yes, thanks. I hope your wife won't mind, I

used her comb and brush. Do you think my clothes are dry? I really should get home.' She knew she was babbling, but she couldn't seem to stop the words from tumbling out. She glanced up to see that sensual mouth quirked in a half smile.

'Let's go see, shall we? And, Jessica, I'm not married.' He appeared to be amused at her clumsy attempts to gain information.

Her heart soared for a moment, then sank at his next statement.

'Not yet, anyway.' He started towards the arch and she followed.

'D-Do you plan to marry soon?' She couldn't look at him, but she had to know.

He glanced back at her speculatively and hesitated before he answered. 'I hope very soon, if she'll have me.'

Jessica's spirits plunged lower, but she said with forced gaity, 'My goodness, your girl-friend must be sensational for you to be so impatient!' Her voice fell when she added, 'I'm sure she'll have you.'

'She is sensational, and I am impatient,' he mused. 'But I don't want to rush her. You see, I've loved her from the first moment I saw her, but we don't know each other very well and she might not feel the same way.'

Why wouldn't she? thought Jessica. I did. She fought to hold back the tears when she said, 'I'm sure she will.'

'I hope so,' he answered, leading her back across the living room.

What would she be like, this girl that Adam loved? Would she be a dainty doll? One thing was certain—she wouldn't be a ragged tomboy! Virility radiated from him in waves and she was sure he attracted the opposite sex like bees to honey. He could pick and choose.

They walked through the swinging door into a shining modern kitchen. Stainless steel and rich walnut cabinets were on three walls. The fourth was sliding glass doors like the living room, to the deck overlooking the ocean.

Although the clock on the wall told her it was early afternoon, the day had darkened to duck.

Jessica approached the wall of glass. Rain was still falling in sheets. The grey-green of the ocean met the grey clouds to blur the horizon. The colours matched her mood. She should have realized that a man like Adam wouldn't be unattached. Her heart was heavy. She needed to get away from here, to go home, where she might be able to face these unfamiliar emotions objectively.

Adam opened the clothes dryer and put his hand inside. 'They're still damp.' He pushed a button to start the tumbling motion again.

There was a huge lump in Jessica's throat. She tried to swallow as she turned from the doors to watch him.

Even though their simultaneous recognition on

the beach had encouraged a certain familiarity, there were still too many unanswered questions, too many doubts, especially with the state of affairs concerning Dennis. She would have to be very careful.

Adam moved gracefully for such a large man. Like a seasoned athlete, he was totally in control of every muscle in that hard body. He lifted the percolator and poured coffee into earthenware mugs. 'Do you take cream or sugar?'

'No, just black.'

Crossing the room with both mugs in his hands, he offered her one.

She took it carefully, concealing her eyes in the steam rising from the hot coffee. She had to calm this fullness in her heart before she looked at him. After all, he was soon going to ask the girl he loved to marry him. A traitorous voice spoke out: 'But he hasn't asked her yet.'

Jessica searched her mind for an innocuous subject. 'The room you put me in is lovely. Did your—er—girl-friend decorate it for you?' So much for an innocuous subject, she thought wryly as she stumbled over the words.

'My father died four years ago. My mother has moved to Atlanta, but spends a month here with me every summer. It's her room,' he answered quietly.

Jessica felt him move to face her and struggled with the urge to meet his eyes.

'Did you really think that if I had a wife she'd

be sleeping in another room?' He sounded amused.

She didn't allow her eyes to lift beyond the hand holding the coffee. His question had conjured up pictures—pictures that were sweet torture, those big hands, gentle on a woman's body, warm, lovingly caressing. She squeezed her eyes tightly shut and forced the pictures from her mind.

'Well, I don't know do I? I don't know you at all.' She resented the sensuality that crept into his tone.

His voice hardened slightly. 'You don't?' he asked.

She turned back towards the window. 'No. You know my name. You say you know my brother, but Dennis isn't here to verify that. You force me into your house—take my clothes; and in an extremely high-handed manner start ordering me around. I don't even know why I allowed it!' she told him sharply.

'That's a good question? Why did you allow it?' he questioned silkily.

She took a deep breath and let it out slowly. Her throat was suddenly too dry for her to answer.

'Look at me, Jess,' he said huskily, using her brother's nickname for her.

Surely it was safe. She faced him and raised disturbed eyes to the darkening grey of his.

Adam inhaled sharply. He took the mug from

her unresisting fingers, and his expression held her prisoner as he set both of them on the table. 'Jess?' he questioned softly. 'Jess . . . on the beach. Did you . . .' His voice trailed off.

Jessica couldn't speak through the obstruction in her throat. She just looked at him helplessly.

He smiled into her upturned face, then his hand went to the fastener in her hair. When he released it the golden silkiness tumbled free over his hand. 'Your hair is beautiful,' he murmured. 'Wear it down for me.' He put the barrette in the pocket of his trousers.

Jessica knew she should protest, but she couldn't. She was mesmerised by the magic of the moment.

With his eyes still holding hers, Adam reached around and, dividing her hair in the back, brought it forward over her shoulder. Tangling his fingers in the strands, he used it easily to draw her closer. 'I'm going to kiss you. When Dennis calls you can ask him if that's okay, too.'

Not a hand's width separated them and yet, except for Adam's hands in her hair, they didn't touch. It was as if they were both revelling in the anticipation of something miraculous. This was a section out of time, a sphere of experience which followed no rules.

Moaning softly, Jessica swayed towards him, and at the same time his hand went to her waist, pulling her finally into the warmth of his arms. A rush of feeling threatened to overcome her. She closed her eyes as his mouth covered hers with sensual mastery. This was where she belonged. His arms held her close, closer than she had ever been to anyone, while he explored her parted lips, her mouth, with gentle thoroughness. His hands moulded her, fitting her to the length of him. His kiss deepened, flamed, lighting fires she didn't know existed.

Jessica's arms curved around his neck. Her fingers buried themselves in his springy hair, loving the feel of it.

The telephone shrilled sharply. With a groan Adam pulled his lips away but still held her. On the second ring he rested his forehead against hers and sighed. He kept her in one arm, close to his broad chest, and reached for the phone on the wall.

Jessica tilted her head back to look up at his strong features in profile. The kiss had left her weak and she leaned heavily on him.

'Yes, who is it?' he said impatiently into the receiver.

She could hear laughing words. Then he paused.

'God! Dennis, I'm sorry! Where the hell are you?' Adam's eyes met Jessica's and his arm tightened. He gave her a rueful grin. 'Great—but try to call in more often. There are a lot of people who were very worried. And speaking of them, I have a surprise for you. I rescued a waif on the beach during a storm about an hour ago.'

Had it only been an hour? Impossible, that an hour ago she hadn't known Adam existed. She felt that she had known him for ever.

'She was wearing one of your old Harvard sweat-shirts. I'll let you talk to her in a minute, but first, what's going on?' He listened intently.

Jessica could hear her brother's voice but couldn't make out the words. She watched, with growing dismay, Adam's face pale, then harden.

'He could blow your cover if he gets too nervous!' He listened again. 'No, we won't take that chance, Dennis. Just get out of there and come back.'

Her brother seemed to be arguing. Adam's arm dropped away from Jessica and the fingers of one hand went to his forehead, rubbing back and forth. His total concentration was on the conversation. 'Let me think a minute.'

She gripped damp palms together. What was going on?

Adam's hand fell to his side. He seemed to have reached some kind of decision. 'Can you get to the island?'

Dennis must have given an affirmative answer, because Adam bit out, 'Okay, get over there and call me back on the short wave. If your contact wants to go with you, take him. I'll see what I can do from this end. Here's Jessica.' He put the receiver into her trembling hand.

'Dennis, I've been so worried! Where are you? When are you coming home?' As she spoke Adam moved away. She shivered at his solemn expression, and tried to keep her mind on her brother's words.

'Hey, Jess, slow down!' Dennis's strong, familiar voice sounded jubilant. 'I'm winding it up here and will be home soon, but I can't tell you when. We've cracked this case and it's really going to split some political rock! But, honey, I only had time for one call, and I was going to have Adam get in touch with Mom and Dad, and you.' His voice was suddenly serious. 'You can trust Adam, Jess,' he said. Then there was amusement, as he went on, 'I thought he might be just the distraction you needed, to get you away from Kevin Short's group. Was I right?'

Her brother had made no pretence of liking Kevin. He was the real estate agent and land owner, who had sold her parents their home. The crowd she had met through him were seemingly on a constant round of parties. She thought them rather shallow and superficial, but they had been friendly and made her feel welcome.

Adam had come back to hold her and, standing close in the circle of his arm, she blushed and groped for a reply. 'Dennis, Mother and Dad are . . .' Suddenly she heard the hiss of his sharply drawn breath and he cursed. There was the sound of a truck in the background. His voice deepened as he interrupted her, 'Jess, my contact is here—I've got to go. But first, give me Adam, quick!'

Evidently Adam heard. He took the phone from her and listened.

Spasmodically his arm tightened. 'They took what!' he exploded.

Seconds dragged as Dennis kept talking.

Adam was grim. 'Don't worry. They'll get to her over my dead body,' he growled.

Jessica could hear laughter in her brother's voice, but not the words.

'I know I said an hour! Now get off this phone and get hell out of there!' Adam slammed down the receiver.

Releasing her, he walked over to stare out of the window. Long fingers raked through his hair. His hand came to rest on the back of his neck and he leaned his head back to fix his gaze on the ceiling. Exhaling on a long sigh, he muttered, 'Damn!'

'Something's terribly wrong, isn't it, Adam?' Jessica asked through numb lips. 'Is Dennis in danger?'

Adam didn't turn, but he spoke calmly, to reassure her. 'We aren't taking any chances with his safety, Jess. You heard me tell him to get out of there. He didn't want to, but he will!' He paused. 'There's something else we have to worry about right now.'

Jessica regarded him dubiously. 'What?'

He took a deep breath and turned to face her. 'I'll explain in a minute. But first, Jess, how much has Dennis told you about this case?'

'Not much. He told me not to discuss his absence with anyone. He made me promise—that's why I didn't mention it to you. I do know that it concerns the drug traffic along the coast.'

'Come here and sit down. I'm going to tell you some more about it.'

They sat facing each other across the table. Almost like adversaries, thought Jessica.

'Dennis was calling from a truck stop about forty miles from here. He's supposed to be a trucker, looking for a job. One of his contacts is a driver who travels this area. He knows everything that goes on within a hundred-mile radius of here and we've tried to enlist his help before. With his testimony we could put a lot of people behind bars, but he hasn't wanted to get involved. Lately, some very unpleasant characters have been paying a lot of attention to him, and he's beginning to get nervous.

'Dennis thinks the man is honest. He felt the time was right to tell him who he really is, and ask him to testify. So he did. I have to go along with your brother's intuition.'

Adam rose, picking up the mugs, and walked to the sink. He poured out the cold coffee and refilled them from the percolator.

Jessica watched him, but when he set her coffee in front of her, she dropped her eyes, afraid of what she would see. She picked up the mug and took a hasty sip of the scalding brew.

Adam sat down opposite her again. 'Dennis has

done an excellent job,' he said almost conversationally. Then his tone hardened. 'With one damn fool exception!'

She stared at him, open-mouthed.

He leaned back in his chair and folded his arms across his chest. He looked very stern. 'These smugglers are suspicious of any stranger, and they've searched Dennis's room. The folder with the pictures of you and your parents was the only thing they took, and that's our worry now.'

Jessica was bewildered. 'I don't understand. What do you mean?'

'Jess, your father is a well known man. These people will show the pictures around, and sooner or later someone will recognise him. They'll dig deeper, wondering why an out-of-work truck driver has pictures of a famous lawyer and his family. And you can be sure they'll eventually find out that the lawyer has a son in the Justice Department.'

Adam took a swallow of coffee. 'Dennis and his team will have to speed up the operation. Even then it will take some time to finish.' He leaned across the table to clasp her cold hand in his. 'You and your parents are going to have to take a vacation until this is over,' he told her.

Jessica frowned and shook her head, still trying to grasp the point. 'We can't,' she said in a small voice.

'You don't have a choice,' he informed her harshly.

She shook her head searching for an alternative. 'You don't understand . . .'

He erupted from his chair. Circling the table, he lifted her roughly by the shoulders. 'You're going if I have to shove you on the plane myself!' Then he groaned and pulled her into his arms. 'The fool! To leave his Justice identification, and take that damned folder!' He rasped against her hair, 'Jess, don't you see? I can't take a chance with your safety.'

She pushed at his chest, and he dropped his arms. Turning half away from her, he pushed his hands into the pockets of the brown slacks.

'Adam, look at me,' she said, as he had said to her earlier.

He seemed reluctant to meet her eyes.

'Why did Dennis call your house? Why here?' Her voice was a husky whisper when she asked, 'Who are you, Adam?'

CHAPTER TWO

'I'm Dennis's boss at the Justice Department.' Adam answered Jessica's question evenly, but his eyes pleaded for her understanding. 'I planned this operation, Jess. I put you and your family in jeopardy.'

She shook her head, not wanting to believe what he was telling her.

'Yes. Of course, Dennis knew he shouldn't have taken the picture with him, but the ultimate responsibility is mine, since I'm in charge.' His voice was grave and he searched her face for a moment before moving wearily back to his side of the table.

He sat down. 'Dennis and I were in law school together. When he came to Justice I knew he was exactly the kind of man we needed for this case.'

Jessica resumed her seat, too and clasped her fingers together, resting her elbows on the table, watching him.

'You see, Jess, I was born in this county. I'd lived here all my life before I moved to Washington. I still have this home, where I spend as much time as possible. Uncles, aunts, and cousins are all over Glynn County. I couldn't take the case myself because too many people know me.'

'But it's vitally important, Jess. The drug traffic must be stopped. These animals must be caught and, more important, prosecuted and convicted so they won't just start up again somewhere else.' He raised his head and looked at her. His eyes were bleak. 'I had to have the best man, and Dennis is the best!'

A chill went through her. She had this awful premonition that Adam was trying to tell her something she didn't quite understand. The fear for her brother had become so much a part of every waking minute over the last few weeks that she had learned to live with it. She had spirit and she refused to look beyond tomorrow, until all this was over, and he was home safely.

Now, however, there was a new dimension to her fear. 'I've been afraid for Dennis. Very afraid.' Her voice was a whisper. 'Should I be afraid now for you, too? And my parents, and myself?' she asked.

'No!' He raked a hand through his hair. 'There's no danger to me.' He dismissed the thought carelessly. 'Your parents and you have to go away—far away where you'll be safe. And I'll take care of you, Jess. I swear that nothing will happen to you,' he said forcefully.

'And Dennis?' she asked.

'How can I possibly answer that? He has everything in the way of back-up that we can provide. He's smart, tough, and in top physical condition. I have confidence that all will go according to plan. But, Jess, I didn't coerce him into taking this job. He felt as strongly about it as I do, and he volunteered.' Adam reached for her hands. 'Dennis would be the first one to tell you that he believes in what he's doing. The drug traffic must be stopped, whatever the risk.' He turned one hand over and caressed the palm with his fingertips. 'Do you understand what I'm saying, Jess?' he asked huskily.

She answered honestly, 'Most of it, I think. I do know that Dennis is something of a daredevil.' When he met her eyes she smiled at him.

Adam heaved a great sigh of relief. 'That he is! But it's what makes him so valuable to the department. Dennis is an idealist who wants to get in there and make things happen, and usually does!' He grinned at her. 'Now, I'll get your clothes.' He used her hand to pull her to her feet and led her to the dryer. Removing her things, he thrust them into her arms. 'Get dressed,' he ordered with a smile. 'I have a few calls to make, then I'll take you home and explain this to your parents. You can decide where you want to go and the Department will make all the arrangements for you. I would suggest a long cruise.' He took her barrette from his pocket and handed it to her.

She choked out a hollow laugh. 'That's exactly where they are!'

'What? Where who are?' he frowned.

'My parents. They've rented a small sailboat and are touring the Greek Islands. They're both avid sailors and this has been a lifelong dream of theirs.'

'Do you mean that you're alone in that house?' he demanded sharply.

'Of course. Our housekeeper is visiting her daughter while Mother and Dad are away.' Her chin came up. 'I'm perfectly capable of taking care of myself.'

'Well, we'll have to get in touch with them. You can fly over and join their cruise.'

'I'm not leaving! How could you possibly think

I would leave?' She was resentful. 'I'm not a child, Adam.'

Adam grabbed her shoulders and turned her to face him fully. 'Stop it! You're going!' As he looked at her, the grip of his hands gentled and became a caress on her upper arms. 'We have a lot to talk about, Jess. But it will have to wait until this is over. I can't take a chance with your safety—it's suddenly become very important to me.'

Her mouth was dry. The look in his eyes turned her bones to water.

His gaze focused on her parted lips, then dropped to the loosened neckline of the robe. As though he couldn't help himself, he lowered his head and his lips were warm on the upper curve of her breast. Then they moved to her mouth in a brief hard kiss before he let her go. 'Get dressed, Jessica,' he said hoarsely.

Jessica was thoroughly shaken and it took her a moment to come down to earth. She finally got the words out. 'Adam, I can't join them. Even if I could I wouldn't, but I really can't!'

He had picked up the telephone, but at her statement he replaced it slowly. 'What are you talking about?' he asked.

'They're "sailing where the four winds take them", as Dad says. They have no itinerary and I have no idea when they'll be home. They call home occasionally, but I never know when.'

Dreading her answer, he asked, 'When did you last hear from them?'

She answered meekly, 'Yesterday.'

'I might have known!' he muttered in disgust.

'Now, I'll get dressed.' Her gleaming hair fanned over her shoulders as she whirled to leave the room.

A sense of urgency hurried her to the bedroom to dress. She was sure that he would try to think of another way to get her out of the area, and she didn't want to leave. She wanted to be here in case . . . in case . . . Quickly she veered her thoughts away from that direction.

She pulled on her jeans, then her hands stilled, remembering the magical moment that Dennis's call had interrupted. The dropping of a golden leaf from a tree, as quickly as it drifts to the ground, a life could change for ever, a love be found. She knew that no matter what happened her life would never be the same.

Forcing herself to move again, she automatically zipped her jeans and impatiently yanked the sweat-shirt over her head. How could she respond so readily when Adam had told her he was marrying soon? Maybe he wanted a last fling, but that wasn't her style. Regret flooded her heart, leaving it aching and empty. She had to fight the response that threatened to drown her in its deluge. But, that traitorous voice in her brain was back, Adam responded, too. Remembering the feel of his hands in her hair, his lips on hers, she knew that he wanted her, but she also knew that she couldn't settle for a temporary physical satisfaction.

Adam was still talking on the phone when she re-entered the kitchen. Cradling the receiver on his shoulder, he made notes as he talked, on a pad held in one hand. He glanced up, but Jessica couldn't read his expression.

In her wrinkled clothes, she felt only slightly more in control of herself. Still, they were dry and she had once again put her hair up.

Finishing his conversation abruptly, he hung up, and stood studying her. 'Jess, what am I going to do with you? I remember Dennis saying that you have no close relatives.' His voice was dogged. 'Is there a friend you can stay with until Dennis gets back?'

Jessica's chin came up and there was a stubbornness in her jaw. 'If there was, I wouldn't tell you, Adam. I'm not leaving.'

'Well, you're sure as hell not going back to that house alone! I can think of only one alternative.'

'What?' she asked warily. Apprehension grew as she watched him turn again to the phone.

'You'll have to stay here.' His face was like stone.

'Here? But I can't! Not here!' she cried.

He ignored her pleading voice and spoke into the phone. 'Grace, this is Adam. You're going to have to rob the house we talked about,' he said hollowly. 'I'm putting Jessica on the line. She can give you directions and tell you what she'll need for a couple of weeks.' He handed the receiver to Jessica. 'Jess, this is Grace Devoe. She's one of our investigators. She'll go to your house, get what you need, and bring it here. Tell her what to pack,' he said firmly.

She took it in numb fingers. 'Adam, I can't. Please, I can't!' she whispered.

He paid no attention. He started through the swinging door to the living room, but stopped. 'And tell her where to find your birth certificate.'

'My birth certificate? For heaven's sake, why?'

'Just tell her!' Adam ordered sharply, and left the room.

When Jessica had finished, she stood for a moment thinking furiously. There had to be another way out. She couldn't possibly stay in this house with Adam. She couldn't! It would be only a matter of time before he recognised how deeply her feelings went, and she could imagine his embarrassment. A man like Adam probably had dozens of girls fall in love with him. Well, she would not be one of the string who had to be let down lightly after a brief affair.

Mentally she checked through a list of close friends. She could hardly stand the thought of going far away until Dennis's safety had been resolved, but there was no refuge in staying in this house!

Jessica's best friend, Leslie, had been married only a short while. Remembering the wedding where she had been maid-of-honour, she smiled wistfully. Certainly she couldn't intrude on a honeymoon. Theresa was in Paris, studying for an advanced degree. Joanne worked for the Embassy in Tokyo. Wildly Jessica searched her mind, and rejected one after the other.

Finally, clenching her fists in frustration, she went into the living room. 'Adam, I've racked my brains and I just can't think of anyone!'

Adam was putting another log on to the fire. Straightening, he dusted his hands off and replaced the brass screen, then held out his hand. 'Come here, Jess.'

Moving with unconscious grace towards him, she put her hand in his. He steered her to the sofa and pulled her down beside him, still holding her hand. His head bent as he studied her palm.

She looked at his lowered head. The dark hair was almost an irresistible temptation to her fingers.

Suddenly he looked at her and she lowered her eyes quickly, but not quickly enough to miss the gleam in his. 'Jess, what did Dennis say to you about me?' he asked.

She blushed, remembering her brother's admitting to matchmaking. 'He—er—he said I could trust you, Adam.'

'And do you?'

'Yes, I do.' She met his eyes. 'I don't know much about you, but for some reason, I do trust you. Of course, I have some questions . . .'

'Fire away!' He dropped her hand and leaned back, crossing his arms across the broad chest.

'Well, you said you're from here, but you work

for the Justice Department. What do you do there? And why did Dennis call you?'

'I'm Dennis's contact on this case. He calls in at prearranged times to report or to ask for back-up. I decided to handle this one personally because I feel strongly about it, and because I'm known in Glynn County. Another stranger nosing around this area might bring on unnecessary suspicion.'

'How . . . how much longer do you think it will be before Dennis comes home?' she asked, a slight quaver in her voice.

'Let me ask you a question before I answer that. What do you think about what Dennis is doing, Jessica? Is it worth the risk?'

She was taken aback for a moment. Her eyes met his with a puzzled frown. No one in Jessica's family ever asked her opinion about anything of importance. She was the baby sister. Her parents and Dennis were loving and protective, and very much convinced that they know what was best for her. So Adam's question was a surprise. 'I'm sure Dennis would think so,' she answered hesitantly.

'But you? What do you think?' He pressured her for an answer and for some unaccountable reasons she was pleased.

'I agree, Adam. I think it's worth the risk,' she told him, lifting her chin positively. 'It may be a dirty job, but it must be done.'

Adam smiled, as at a pupil who had done

particularly well. 'Then you agree that we should do whatever we can to find these people and bring them to justice?'

She nodded in agreement.

'No matter how long it takes?' He took her hand in his again. 'That's the answer to your question, Jess. Dennis will be home when it's over,' he said gently. 'I know it's hard for you, to be alone like this.'

She sighed. 'Well, Dennis didn't know the folks were leaving and they didn't know what he was doing, so . . .'

'So that leaves me.' He took a deep breath. 'Do you believe me when I tell you that you're in danger, Jess?'

Her throat tightened and she nodded. 'But, Adam . . .'

He interrupted. 'As I said before, your father is a well known man. The feature writers on the local paper had a heyday when he retired from his firm in Washington and moved here. There were pictures of the three of you. Fortunately I was able to squelch any of Dennis. But, Jessica, if the people who stole the pictures got to you, Dennis could be forced into an impossible choice.' He spoke slowly, giving her time to realise his meaning. 'Now, do you understand?'

'Yes,' she answered softly. 'I would be sort of a hostage. Is that what you mean?'

His mouth twisted. 'Sort of.'

'I do understand, Adam, when you explain it

like that. But I can't go to my parents. I don't know where they are,' she said with a break in her voice. 'And I don't have anyone else.'

'There's me.'

'No! No, I'm not staying here! You could give me a bodyguard, or something!'

'I am giving you a bodyguard—me. I can't spare the people it would take, Jess, but since I'm not out in the field on this one anyway . . .'

'What if I dye my hair? I could pretend to be the maid at home.'

Adam dropped the hand he had held and stood, thrusting his fists into his pockets. 'You've been reading too many mysteries.' He turned his back. 'I thought you trusted me, Jess.'

'I do. But there has to be another answer. You talked about the newspapers. I can't move in here with you! My parents—I . . . I just can't.' Her shoulders drooped.

Adam answered quietly, his voice emotionless, 'You could if we were married, Jess.'

If he had dropped a tiger in her lap, Jessica would not have been more stunned. She looked at him, her eyes as big as saucers. 'Married!' She stood with a jerk and began to pace. 'Married? You're crazy!' Stopping in front of him, she looked up into those hard grey eyes, and her tone softened. 'We can't get married! We barely know each other, and besides, what would your . . . the girl you're going to marry, what would she say?' Her heart was like lead in her chest. Not like this. Please, not like this, she cried inside.

Adam looked at her steadily until she was forced to drop her eyes. 'The girl I plan to marry,' he said heavily. 'Well, I'll admit I'm taking a chance. But I hope, I pray, that the girl I love will understand some day why I'm doing what I'm doing.'

'That's asking rather a lot of her,' Jessica said dryly.

'I hope not. It won't be for ever. We'll monitor the calls at your house. When the case is wrapped up and your parents are back home, we can have the marriage annulled.'

'Annulled?'

'You didn't think I'd take advantage of the situation, did you?' For the first time there was a gleam of something—amusement?—in his eyes. He gave her a mock bow. 'You may have my mother's room.'

'Thank you! My mind is relieved to know that!' While my heart is breaking, she added to herself. Oh, Adam!

Four hours later Jessica's head was spinning as they walked out of the house of the minister who had just pronounced that they were man and wife. The kindly man, his wife, and their grown son, who lived next door, had been the only witnesses at her wedding. She choked back a sob, and Adam's hand tightened on her shoulder. He thanked the minister and led her to the small blue sports car.

As he closed the door for her she looked at the heavy gold of the old-fashioned wedding band on her finger. It had been his grandmother's. She must have been tiny, because her own hands were small and it fitted snugly.

Adam got in beside her and slipped the key into the ignition, but before starting the engine he turned to look at her. 'Are you all right, Jess?' he asked gently.

'I'm fine! I meet a man after lunch and before dinner I'm married to him. Why shouldn't I be fine?' Her voice was shaky as she struggled for composure. Married! And to someone she knew she was in love with . . . she almost laughed out loud. This had to be the Number One farce of all time!

Adam had been adamant that this was the only way to protect both her person and her reputation. He felt responsible for her, and she didn't want that! She wanted something different, very different.

'But did it have to be a minister?' she whispered so low that he had to lean close to hear. 'Couldn't we have just gone to City Hall?'

He straightened and his hands tightened convulsively on the wheel, his knuckles white, but when he answered her his voice was even and controlled. 'City Hall is closed for the night! Jessica, this situation is difficult enough as it is. Please try to make the best of it.'

'I'm sorry, Adam.' There were tears in her

eyes. 'I know you had more to lose than I did. I'll try not to be any trouble.' Her voice broke on the last word. Tears streamed down her face. 'It's just that this isn't exactly what I imagined my wedding would be like.' He groaned and turned to lift her across to his lap and cradle her in his arms like a child. 'Okay, baby, cry it all out.' His tenderness released a flood. His arms were strong and comforting as they held her, but his eyes were full of pain. His big hand clasped her head to his shoulder, but she was oblivious to the soft touch of his lips on her forehead.

When she finally began to control her sobs, Adam lifted her face with a finger under her chin. He took a snowy white handkerchief from his pocket and dried her eyes. 'Is that better?' he asked with a sad smile.

Nodding, Jessica answered with a gulp, 'I cried all over your shirt.' She plucked the damp material away from his hard chest, before looking up at him.

He smoothed a wayward strand of hair back from her face. 'You know,' he said huskily, 'I didn't kiss the bride.'

Jessica held her breath, remembering the moment at the end of the short service. She had turned to him. He had smiled that heartwarming smile, and his hand had gripped hers tightly, but he hadn't kissed her.

But now his eyes dropped to her trembling lips. Slowly he bent his head to cover them with his. The kiss was unbelievably tender and gentle. She touched his cheek and felt the muscles in his jaw tense.

Abruptly Adam broke off the kiss and settled her back in her own seat. Her lower lip trembled in response to the withdrawal, but she clamped her teeth on it quickly.

As he started the car, Adam asked, 'Are you hungry?'

Jessica looked at him in surprise. He was pale under his tan, but he grinned.

Unsettled by the kiss, she had to swallow before she could answer him. 'I'm starved!' she said although she had never felt less like eating in her life.

Adam took a deep breath and let it out slowly. 'Well, that's a situation we can do something about.'

Jessica had a chance to study him as he reversed the car and manoeuvred on to the highway. From the grim-faced man who had repeated the marriage vows, he seemed determined to lighten the atmosphere between them. She was swamped with guilt. He didn't want this any more than she did, and she could at least make an effort to make herself less of a burden to him.

'I'm going to take you to the greatest little seafood spot on this coast,' Adam told her. 'They have raw oysters and boiled shrimp that aren't to be topped. Of course, you have to open and peel them yourself, but they bring you a bucket of water to wash afterwards.'

She managed a lilt in her voice when she joked back, 'Do you think we're dressed for it? This sounds like an elegant spot.'

The car stopped for a red light, and Adam looked at her smooth chignon of blonde hair. His eyes fell to the white chiffon dress, lingering for a moment on her breasts, before continuing down the length of her long legs to the high-heeled sandals. Jessica was shaking inside by the time his gaze reached her toes.

'As a matter of fact, as luscious as you look, you'd probably fit in better as my waif of this afternoon.'

His casual perusal had unnerved her again, but she forced herself to be casual, suggesting, 'Then let's go home and change first.'

'Home?' He raised an eyebrow and pulled into the traffic.

'I'm sorry, Adam.' She blushed and added in a more subdued tone, 'I meant to your house, of course.'

'I'm glad you said home. It sounds better.' Reaching over, he covered her hand with his. 'It is your home, Jess.'

She withdrew her fingers and turned to stare out of the window. 'For the time being. Maybe it won't be too long, Adam. I know you want to get this over with.'

He muttered something under his breath.

Jessica couldn't hear what he said, but thought it best not to ask him to repeat it.

'Mmm, Adam, the Oyster Bar is everything you promised.' Jessica dried her hands on one of the bright blue towels they had been given instead of napkins. She had changed into white slacks and a blouse which reflected the violet blue of her eyes. Leaning back in her chair, she sighed in contentment. Adam was really a very good-looking man, she reflected, watching him pop the last oyster into his mouth. The Madras slacks and yellow knit shirt fitted him like a second skin. Her husband! Suddenly her mouth was dry. Each time he reached out to pick up his wine glass she was mesmerised by the play of muscle under his shirt. Remembering the strength of his arms carrying her across the dunes, she allowed her imagination rein to pretend that this was a real marriage. When they got home he would lift her over the threshold and begin to kiss her as he carried her down the hall . . . She longed for those arms around her again.

Adam looked up and surprised her gaze. The light from the patio candle reflected in his eyes and she couldn't read his expression, but he put his arm along the back of her chair and leaned towards her. His broad shoulders blocked her from the rest of the room. His deep voice was husky as he murmured for only her ears, 'You're so damned beautiful! Do you have any idea what you do to a man when you look at him like that?' His finger traced her jawline and came to rest at a spot just below her ear.

Jessica shivered and dropped her eyes to the top button of his shirt. Nervously she took a breath and moistened her dry lips.

'God, Jess!' he rasped. His hand tightened on the side of her neck.

She raised her eyes questioningly.

A man approached their table and, as he spoke, Adam reluctantly tore his gaze from her mouth and removed his hand.

'Adam! I didn't know you were in town. Why haven't you called?' He greeted Adam with a big smile on his thin face. He was not much taller than Jessica, and very slim. Deep laughter lines scored his face.

Adam stood to shake hands with him. 'I'm in and out, Andy. Jess, I'd like for you to meet Andy Flowers. He owns the Oyster Bar. Andy, this is my wife, Jessica.' His voice was unsteady.

'Your wife?' Andy's stupefied expression was no more surprised than Jessica's. 'You old son of a gun!' He clapped Adam on the back heartily. 'So you're finally going to give the other fellers around here a chance, huh? I'm glad to meet you, Jessica.' He reached for her hand and shook it enthusiastically.

She struggled to regain her poise. 'I'm happy to meet you, too, Andy. The food was delicious.'

'Thanks. I hope you'll come often. And

congratulations to you both.' He moved away in response to a call from another table.

Adam resumed his seat. 'Andy is a drop-out,' he told her with a solemn smile.

'A drop-out?'

He nodded. 'Andy and his wife and daughter Annie lived in Atlanta. He was a very successful accountant, but it was big city life and it was hectic. The pressures were there, but Andy could have handled those. Until his daughter began to associate with a pretty wild bunch of youngsters, and one day he found drugs in her room. She was only fourteen years old. So Andy quit his job and moved his family down here, hoping for a quieter and more wholesome life for Annie. They started this restaurant and it's been a booming success, mainly because they all pitch in. Lately, though, Annie has begun to worry them again.' He paused and met her eyes. 'She's going around with Kevin Short's crowd.'

Jessica was surprised at the grimness in his tone. 'How old is she now?'

'She's seventeen.'

'Well, I agree, she's much too young for their brand of sophistication; but, Adam, I've gone around some with that crowd, too. I know Dennis doesn't like them, but Kevin has been friendly and introduced me to a lot of his friends. They enjoy partying a bit too much, but I don't think there's any real harm in them.'

Adam's face hardened. If she hadn't known

better, Jessica would have said that he sounded almost jealous when he said, 'I didn't realise you'd be so defensive of him. All I know is that he isn't too particular about some of the people he associates with.' He rose. 'Let's go.'

When they had left the restaurant, Jessica tried to regain the happier atmosphere they had shared during dinner. She looked up at the stars. The weather had cleared miraculously and it was a beautiful night. 'That was a memorable meal, Adam. I don't know when I've eaten so much.'

Adam opened the car door for her, but he gripped her arm for a moment before putting her in. 'I'm glad it was memorable, Mrs Oakman. As a nuptial dinner it wasn't typical, but I'd be willing to bet you won't forget it.'

She ducked her head and slid into the car. If only he wouldn't keep referring to their marriage, she thought, maybe her heart would quiet to a steadier beat.

They returned to the rock and glass house at a leisurely pace, savouring the beauty of the night. Jessica had relaxed by the time they entered the house, and Adam locked the door behind them. 'Shall I make some coffee?' she asked as he walked to the desk and picked up the telephone.

'That would be good. Do you think you can find everything?' He had dialled a number and spoke tersely into the receiver. 'We're back.'

She glanced back in surprise. 'What was that about?' she asked.

'Someone has to know where I am at all times, Jess. Come on, I'll show you where the coffee is.'

While they waited for it to perk Jessica went over to the glass door. She looked out into the darkness towards the ocean. 'The sea is wonderful. The surf seems to glow with its own light,' she remarked.

He chuckled. 'Not very romantic, I'm afraid. That's the phosphorus in the water. Wait a minute, let me show you something.'

She jumped when he flicked the switch to plunge the room into darkness. 'Adam, what are you doing?'

'Look out again, Jess.' He came to stand behind her. His hands on her shoulders turned her towards the scene outside.

'Oh—h!' she breathed softly, drinking in the sight. Now the edges of the waves were brighter, reflecting the shimmering glow of a moon somewhere out of sight. As she watched, the patterns continuously changed, producing a ballet of lines and sprays. Unconsciously, she relaxed against Adam. 'It's magnificent, isn't it?'

She felt him stiffen behind her and immediately started to move away, but one of his hands circled her waist to hold her where she was. The other hand went to the pins in her hair, releasing it, before completing the circle. He held her close against him and buried his face in her hair.

'Your hair smells good.' His breath was uneven, his voice husky.

'It's your mother's shampoo,' she said in a muffled shaking voice.

'I must be crazy,' he groaned. 'We've known each other only a few hours, but all I can think about is that this is our wedding night!' A shudder went through him. 'And I'm holding a very sexy wife in my arms.'

Jessica bit her lip. The feel of his arms was heaven, but she had to stop this. 'All I can think about is your fiancée,' she said stiffly.

'Fiancée?' He sounded as though he didn't know what she was talking about.

She tried to wriggle free, but his arms held her firmly.

'Don't, Jess. Be still,' he said hoarsely. 'This is dangerous as hell, but just let me touch you and hold you for a moment.' His lips were sensuously warm, nibbling her neck and the lobe of her ear. 'You're so beautiful!' he rasped as his hands slid upward to caress her breasts through the silk of her blouse.

His breath was warm against her soft skin, setting off unknown flames deep in the pit of her stomach. A soft moan escaped from her throat. Her knees refused to support her and she relaxed against him, unable to resist the breathtaking thrill of his touch. She was abandoned to the desire he aroused with the rhythmic movement of his hands.

'Jess, we've got to talk . . .' he began, his voice a husky murmur.

She whimpered his name and suddenly he did turn her, crushing her to him. Jessica's arms were around his waist, clinging. Willingly she lifted her lips. His mouth made selfish use of hers and she revelled in it.

Adam's hands moved convulsively over her back and down to her hips, drawing her closer. 'God, I want you!' Desire thickened his voice and she trembled in response. She arched to him and felt the muscles of his thighs hardening against her. Her mind had ceased to function and her feelings were totally in control of her body. She ached with longing for him.

Adam shuddered violently and dragged his lips from hers, resting his forehead against her hair. 'No!' he groaned. 'No, I can't. Jess,' he said in that husky voice, 'This is an explosive situation. I can hardly keep my eyes off you, much less my hands.'

'You don't do my equilibrium much good either, Adam,' she murmured. Her fingers were restless on his chest and he covered them with one of his, stilling their movement.

'We'd better have some coffee and discuss it.' He still held her, his hand warm over hers.

Jessica could feel the rapid pounding of his heart, his super human effort to slow his breathing. 'Okay.' She didn't move.

He heaved a sigh and let her go, crossing to turn the light on.

She felt so cold without his arms around her. Gripping her elbows in front of her, she shivered.

When Adam turned back and saw her rumpled hair and swollen lips, and the dazed look in her eyes, his good intentions almost flew out of the window. 'You're so beautifully dishevelled,' he teased unsteadily.

She smiled a little and put up a shaking hand to smooth her hair.

'Don't—I like you that way. You look as if you've been thoroughly kissed.' He started toward her, then stopped. 'Go out to the fire. I'll bring our coffee.'

Her long legs were still unsteady when she crossed the living room to curl up on the sofa.

Adam followed in a moment carrying the coffee. He avoided touching her, and set the mug down on the table. Taking his to the fire, he sat on the raised hearth, elbows resting on his knees. The dying embers sent out a glow to play on the strong planes of his face. The only other light in the room was a small lamp on a chest by the front door.

Jessica's eyes were on his hands, turning the mug as if seeking its warmth. When he lifted it to swallow, she watched the play of muscle in his throat. She wanted to store up visions of him. She was in love for the first time in her twenty-two years and it was an unholy mess, but she wanted these memories no matter what happened. There was a feeling inside her that she would need them. She leaned forward and picked up her coffee.

Adam looked at her and she quickly lowered her eyes. The expression in them must be as simple to interpret as a first-year reader.

Adam's tones were carefully measured when he spoke. 'You're a very sexy lady, Jess.' He paused, then continued, 'And it's impossible for me to forget that we're married, no matter what the circumstances are, or however briefly.' He searched for a reaction, but her face did not betray her turbulent thoughts.

'You're a virgin, aren't you?' he asked blandly.

Jessica couldn't control the blush that flooded her cheeks. She didn't answer, but Adam didn't seem to expect one.

His fingers gripped the mug, and he went on heavily, 'Some day you'll want to walk down the aisle in a white wedding gown to the man you love.'

Her eyes flew to his and she almost cried out loud. To you, only you!

'I don't want you to have any regrets, Jess.' His deep voice was firm. 'We'll have this marriage annulled as soon as the danger is over, then you can go back to your life again. It has to be this way.'

Jessica shivered. Back to what? Her life would never be the same, she knew that. And regrets? Her deepest regret would be if this man went out of her life. But what of his regrets? He was in love with someone. If he made love to her, knowing that he was the first, he might feel that he had to stay married out of a sense of duty, and she knew that she couldn't stand that.

He stood abruptly and turned to stare into the fire. She again allowed herself the luxury of watching the muscular strength of him. But she realised his strength was not all in his well trained body. He was a man of deliberate resolve and determined purpose.

Jessica searched for a way to reassure him. Her response had been so unmistakable. Adam gave her the way when he said, 'I hope some day you'll be able to forgive me for getting you into this mess.'

She raised her chin determinedly. 'You forget, Adam, that I know my brother rather well, It seems to me that he had more to do with getting me into this than you did. Still, I guess I owe him one. He's been pulling me out of scrapes for years.'

'Don't blame Dennis. He's carried that folder for so long, it's probably more of a habit than carrying his driver's licence,' he said wryly. 'In the meantime, I'll try to control myself while you're living here if you'll help. Is it a pact?'

She tried to find the words to deny her feelings, but before she could answer, he whirled back to face her.

'Dammit, Jess, help me out! We've got to live together for a week or two! And we can't do it like this.' His hand raked his hair, and he came down on one knee in front of her, taking the mug from her numb fingers. His voice was low and husky as he put them both down and took her hands. 'I'm a man, Jess, with a healthy appetite.' He let his eyes roam where they would for a brief second. 'And you're the juiciest little morsel I've seen for a long time. I'd very much like to make love to you. But I'm not going to.'

Jessica swallowed the lump in her throat. Denying her love for this wonderful man was the hardest thing she had ever had to do. She forced herself to speak quietly. 'It's all right, Adam, I understand. We were thrown together under unusual circumstances, but you don't love me, and I . . . I don't love you. It would be a big mistake to let ourselves—er—be carried away.' She rose and turned to avoid those eyes. 'We're mature adults, not adolescents unable to control our emotions.'

'Do you believe that, Jess?' he asked with a cheerless smile. 'That speech you just made?'

'Yes! Yes, I do!' She hooked her hair behind an ear and faced him. 'We'll have to take each day as it comes.' My God, she thought to herself, can't I speak in any way but clichés?

He raised an eyebrow and studied her silently for a moment. 'You're exhausted, Jess. Go to bed.'

She nodded and walked to the archway. 'Goodnight, Adam.'

'Goodnight.'

CHAPTER THREE

THE next morning Jessica awoke in the blue and gold room, the sun shining through the windows. Frowning, she raised herself on her elbows and looked around. Then she remembered. Relaxing against the pillows, she sighed. She had been so emotionally drained and exhausted last night that she had tumbled into bed without a thought of closing the curtains. Now she lay in languid reverie watching a seagull trace circles on the blue sky.

What a muddle! Her thoughts drifted back over the past twenty-four hours. The moments on the beach, when it had all begun, flooded her again with the heart-stopping familiarity she had felt on first meeting Adam's eyes. A small smile played around her lips and she lifted her arms to cradle her head in her hands.

The gull dropped out of sight, then was back, climbing up, up towards the sun. Jessica's intuition had turned her in the same way, towards Adam, towards his warmth. There were no doubts in her mind. It did happen outside of novels. She loved him wholly and completely, and for the rest of her life.

She wanted to jump from the bed and run to

find him, to throw herself into his arms and tell him! The pact was forgotten momentarily. Then the bubble of joy burst and she uttered a half-hysterical sob. She couldn't do that . . . she was married to him! For now anyway; and he didn't love her. He was physically aroused by her, she had no doubt about that, but he was in love with a 'sensational girl' . . . and impatient to marry her. A stab of jealousy for the unknown girl went through her. She flopped over and buried her face in the pillow, but the release of tears was denied, and finally she threw back the covers and got out of bed.

As she stood under the refreshing spray of the shower, the moments in the kitchen came back to her. That explosive scene could have easily got out of hand. She would have let Adam make love to her. Blushing, she made herself admit the truth. Let him? She yearned for it. But Adam had seen the pitfalls, and led her around them. He had been gentle but firm when he had sent her to bed, alone.

Well, Dennis couldn't get her out of this predicament. In fact, it very much looked as if he had got her into it! And this time she had to depend on herself!

Jessica dressed in powder blue slacks and a matching velour top with long sleeves and a vee-neck. A touch of mascara and lip-gloss were all the make-up she normally used. Running a brush through her hair, she remembered Adam's fingers tangling in the strands. She leaned to the mirror and looked herself in the eye. Stop it! she instructed, lifting a finger to point at her image. Keep your mind on why you're here. To help Dennis!

She rose from the dressing table and went to the door. As she opened it she heard the clatter of a typewriter and a muffled curse. Lingering at the archway leading to the living room, she looked across to where Adam sat at the desk. His hair had fallen forward over his forehead and he appeared thoroughly exasperated. Jessica smiled to herself tenderly while she watched him.

The typewriter keys stuck again and he exploded, 'Damn!'

She jumped at the imprecation and her movement caught his eye. 'Jess! I didn't know you were awake.' He left the desk and came towards her.

Her breath caught in her throat at the sight of his muscular body in a black knit shirt and white duck pants. She longed to reach up and smooth the wayward lock from his face. This would not do! She clenched her fists, looking away.

'Good morning, Mrs Oakman.'

'Don't! Don't call me that!' She began to tremble, overwhelmingly aware of his virility.

He must have mistaken her emotion, for his arm encircled her shoulder and he said reassuringly, 'I know, I shouldn't remind either one of us, should I? How about "Good morning, Beachcomber"?'

She glanced up to find his eyes jovially bright.

'Come on. We'll get some breakfast for you and maybe you won't be so touchy.'

'I'm not touchy!' she pouted.

He didn't answer but led her to the kitchen and sat her at the table, before going over to pour her a cup of coffee. 'Now, what would you like? I'm a fantastic breakfast cook.'

'Just the coffee, Adam. I'm really not very hungry.'

'Nonsense! You need a good breakfast. One of my Oakman Omelettes will smooth out those rough edges for the day! Are you always such a grouch in the morning?' he teased.

'No! Are you always such a life of the party?' she asked sarcastically. How in the world could he be so cheerful under the circumstances?

He didn't say another word, but hummed to himself and began to clatter pots and pans.

Jessica sipped her coffee, watching the efficiency of his movements. Soon he placed a plate before her. The omelette was light and fluffy, and with it was golden-brown toast.

She ate every bite. 'Adam, that was delicious. I didn't think I was hungry.' She rose and brought her plate over to where he was loading the dishwasher. 'You were right—I do feel better, but I'm stuffed.'

His eyes assessed her curves warmly, 'Yes, you

are. Very nicely stuffed, too.'

She couldn't control a shiver of delight, but reproached him sternly, 'Adam, remember our pact!'

'I apologise, Jess.' He was obviously irritated with himself. 'You're right, of course. But . . . oh, hell! I've got to get back to work.'

Jessica hesitated before she said, 'It's a shame you aren't as good a typist as you are a cook. Would you like some help? I can type.'

'You can? Wonderful! Then you're the answer to a prayer in more ways than one.' He grinned. 'Come with me.' Leading the way back into the living room, he explained, 'I'm working on the budget request for the department. I usually come down here to work when I need peace and privacy. There's a woman, Mrs Scott, who types for me when I'm here, but one of her children is in hospital with appendicitis.'

She mused, 'I would have thought there was a temporary help agency in Brunswick.'

Adam flushed. 'Well, there is one, but they just haven't worked out for me.'

I'll just bet they haven't, thought Jessica. They probably couldn't take their eyes off you for long enough to concentrate. I'd better watch myself or I'll be doing the same thing, she added to herself. She sat down at the typewriter and put in a fresh piece of paper.

Adam leaned over her shoulder. 'The lists of figures are here. Can you read what I've written?'

Jessica looked at the papers. His handwriting was bold and black. 'No problem.' She started to type briskly and efficiently. After a moment she stopped and looked up. Adam was still standing, staring down at her.

'Thanks, Jess,' he said in a low voice. He turned away and went to the table in front of the sofa, which was piled high with more stacks of papers and several law books. The broad back settled against the cushions, and he reached for a yellow legal-sized pad and a pen.

Jessica made herself concentrate on the figures before her and, for a long time, the only sounds in the room were the crackling of the fire and the clicking of the typewriter keys.

It was about ten o'clock when the telephone rang. Adam answered tersely, then his voice changed. 'Yes, sir!' He listened attentively.

Jessica had turned to watch in surprise at the deep-toned respect. 'We'll probably finish here in a few days, sir.' Another pause. 'Of course. I know you wouldn't ask me to come if it wasn't important. We can be there this afternoon.'

He glanced at Jessica. 'I'll be bringing a passenger, sir—my wife. We were married yesterday.'

Jessica inhaled sharply. Whoever this was that Adam spoke to with such deference shouldn't be told about this marriage! How were they going to have it quietly annulled if he kept announcing it?

'You may know her, sir. She's Daniel Gentry's

daughter, Jessica.' He listened for a few more moments. 'We'll look forward to that. See you at seven, then, sir. Goodbye.'

'Adam! Who was that? Why did you tell him we were married? Does he know my father?' she babbled.

'Hey, slow down!' he laughed. 'One at a time! That was the Attorney-General, and you can be assured that he was aware of our marriage almost before we were. He has an uncanny sense of knowing everything that goes on in the department. How do you think I made the arrangements so quickly?'

'Does . . . does he know the circumstances?' asked Jessica on a plaintive note.

'No. No one does, except Dennis.'

'Dennis! You've talked to Dennis again?' Her blue eyes were huge.

Adam nodded. 'He called from the island—we have a communications base there. I talked to him last night after you'd gone to bed. He's the only one who knows why we married.' He unfolded his long length from the sofa and came over to lean against the desk. 'And that's the way I want it, Jess.'

She realised that this purposeful man would explain himself to no one unless he chose to do so.

'He does know my father,' she said. 'I've often heard Daddy speak of him, but I've never met him.'

Adam watched her closely. 'Well, you'll meet him tonight. He and his wife have invited us for cocktails and dinner, so be sure to pack something appropriate.'

'Pack? Where are we going?' Remembering the earlier part of the conversation, she rose agitatedly, and came around the desk to face him.

'We're flying to Washington—something has come up that I can't handle from here. Don't worry, Jess, our communications system is excellent. The calls here will be re-routed. We won't be out of touch for a minute and we'll be back tomorrow night.' Adam looked down into her face, smiling slightly. A long finger tucked her hair behind an ear.

She moved away. 'I wasn't worried, Adam, I was just thinking . . . wouldn't it be better if I stayed here? I could finish all your typing while you're gone.' And I could have a breathing space, she added to herself, away from the magnetic pull of his attraction.

'No! I am not going anywhere without you!' His tone left no room for argument. 'Now, scat! I want to leave as soon as possible.'

As Jessica folded her clothes and placed them in her suitcase she mused about the coming dinner date with the Attorney-General. She had heard her father mention him a number of times. It was going to be difficult to end this marriage quietly if Adam told everyone, she thought crossly. And her parents . . . what if they heard about it before she had a chance to explain to them? They would be so hurt until they knew the true story.

She stopped in the middle of folding a robe. How wonderful it would be if this were a real marriage! At the thought of Adam's hands on her, making love to her with tender passion, her eyes darkened and shimmered with moisture. She pictured a miniature Adam toddling on the beach, with that same curly hair, those same steady grey eyes and the same heartwarming smile. Adam would make a wonderful father, firm and loving.

'Penny for your thoughts.' The object of those thoughts, standing in the doorway, interrupted her reverie and she started. A blush crept slowly up her face.

'They're worth far more than a penny,' she said, turning back to the suitcase to hide any further blushes, or anything else he might see.

'They must be,' he said. 'You blush so beautifully. Have you finished packing?'

'Yes, this is the last.' Jessica closed the case, grateful that the caressing note was gone from his voice. 'Should I change, Adam? You didn't say what time our flight leaves.'

'It leaves as soon as we get there.' He chuckled at her blank expression. 'I have a plane that I use for commuting, so I'm your pilot, Jess. Are you afraid?'

She looked at him, amazed. 'No-o-o, I'm not

afraid.' Whatever he did he would do well. 'I'm beginning to wonder if there's anything you can't do!' she said lightly.

'Oh, one or two things' he answered. 'Let's go.' Adam picked up the suitcase and she followed him down the hall and out of the house to the car.

The fence around the small airport was almost hidden by huge boxwood hedges. Adam steered the sports car between wide gates and parked beside a small concrete block building. 'There she is!' he pointed to a gleaming plane which stood on the runway. 'That's a Cessna 182, called a Skylane. Isn't she a beauty?' he demanded, his eyes glowing.

Jessica had only been on commercial flights and, unable to match his enthusiasm, looked dubiously at the small aircraft. 'Yes, she's a beauty,' she mumbled.

Adam removed their luggage and locked the car. He led her over to where a man was standing beside the plane.

'All checked out and ready to go, Adam.' The tall, slim man had deep laughter lines in his tanned face, and his hair was completely grey.

'Thanks, Bill.' Adam introduced Bill Moore to Jessica and she responded readily to his sincere smile, but her eyes kept returning to the small aircraft.

'He's a passable pilot' Bill laughed, correctly interpreting her doubt.

'Bill taught me to fly when I was sixteen, Jess.

He had unlimited patience and nerves of steel. I'm afraid I was a headstrong pupil who wanted to do everything "now"!'

She responded to Bill. 'I'm not worried about Adam, but that's such a tiny little plane. Do you really think it will make it?' she asked doubtfully.

They both laughed and Bill took an arm to escort her to the plane. He showed her where to step on the landing gear strut to climb inside, while Adam stowed their suitcases. Jessica was glad she had on her slacks; her entry was less than graceful.

Adam climbed in beside her and leaned over to buckle her in. As he drew away he looked into her eyes. His own were sparkling. Then he leaned over to give her a light kiss. 'You're going to love this, Jess. It gives you a sense of freedom that you get nowhere else. My mother flies, you know.'

'Your mother?' Her surprise covered the confusion wrought by his kiss.

'Yes, she's flown since she was a young girl. I have my instructor's licence. If you want to try it some day I'll teach you.' He grinned at her.

If I'm around, she thought wryly.

As the small plane lifted off the runway, Jess's heart lifted with it. They climbed steadily, and she peered through the side window watching the cars, trees, and buildings grow smaller and smaller. Gradually her clenched fists relaxed. She looked ahead through the windshield to the dazzling blue of the sky dotted with only wisps of clouds. A ribbon of highway below followed their route for a few miles before veering away, and Jessica could see the coastline with its shining beaches and offshore islands gleaming green in the sunlight.

She turned radiant eyes to Adam's. He was watching her reaction and smiling that heart-warming smile. Her own heart flip-flopped in her chest. Excitement brimmed over into gay laughter. 'You're right, Adam! This is nothing like being in an airplane with three hundred other people! Do you really think I could learn?'

'Of course you can. I knew you'd like it,' he said with a self-satisfied grin.

The flight took almost four hours, but to Jessica it seemed far too short. Adam pointed out landmarks as they flew over South Carolina, North Carolina, and Virginia.

They talked easily, filling in blanks of what they knew of each other. Only once did the conversation become stilted. Jessica was reminiscing about growing up in Dennis's shadow. She had wanted to do everything that he did. 'When he told me that he was going to be a fireman when he grew up, I naturally decided that that was what I wanted to be, too. I was going to spend all my days careering around on the back of a hook and ladder truck and never get married!'

Adam answered quietly, 'Well, we put an end to that one, didn't we?'

The smile disappeared from her face and she caught her lower lip between her teeth. She bowed her head to stare at the fingers clasped tensely in her lap.

A warm hand covered her smaller ones and she looked up to find Adam's gaze on her mouth. He raised his eyes to hers and held them.

Her heart was pounding heavily. She could hear the echo in the pulsebeat drumming in her ears.

'A man could drown in those blue eyes,' he grated.

Jessica let her lashes drop to cover the ardent expression she knew was kindled there and swallowed before she spoke. Striving to countermand his serious tone, she said, 'Not while he's flying a plane. I hope.'

He gave her hands a hard squeeze before he let go of them. 'You're right! Not the time or the place.'

Would there ever be a right time or place? Jessica wondered desperately.

They were both silent for a time until Adam casually pointed out the gleaming ribbon of the historic James River below them. They were over Virginia. Soon their conversation was as easy as before.

When they landed at Washington National Airport Jessica thought it was like dropping from a beautiful dream back to reality.

Adam came around the plane to lift her out, both hands at her waist. 'Did you enjoy it?' he asked, grinning down at her.

She laughed, 'I can hardly wait until tommorrow to do it again!'

He held her against him for a moment before reaching for their luggage. She thought she caught a note of tenderness in his voice when he said, 'You have a wonderful capacity for living, don't you, Jess?'

'Except before breakfast?' she teased.

Adam gave a hoot a laughter. 'You're so right! Come on, let's find a cab.'

CHAPTER FOUR

JESSICA had been born and lived all her life in Washington. She felt a swell of homecoming as they crossed the Memorial Bridge into the city itself, and the Lincoln Memorial loomed before them. Shaped like a Greek temple, the huge marble edifice was a fitting tribute to the sixteenth President of the United States. The majesty of it always brought a lump to her throat.

Adam's thoughts must have paralleled hers, because he said, 'Let's stop by the Lincoln Memorial some time before we go back.'

'I'd like that,' said Jessica.

The taxi took them to Georgetown, the oldest and most beautiful of the residential areas surrounding Washington, D.C. As they turned into a familiar driveway, Jessica looked around, a frown between her brows. 'I've been here before,' she said, looking back at the big house they had just passed.

They continued down the drive to a converted carriage house at the back of the property. There the driver got out and came around the car to open the door for her.

'Jeanine Soiret, a girl I was in school with, lived here. Her father was a diplomat from Belgium,' she said.

'In the big house, you mean? Yes, I remember them. They've returned home, and the house is now leased to the Millers from Utah. He came here during this administration to serve in the Department of the Interior.' Adam paid the man, adding a generous tip, as he deposited the luggage on the front step.

'Thank you, sir. If I can be of further service, please ask for Abe Allen.' The driver doffed his cap politely.

Adam looked at him with narrowing eyes. 'Have you driven me before, Abe?'

'Yes, sir, I've had that pleasure several times. You're Mr Oakman, aren't you, sir?' He seemed amused.

'That's right. I have to go out again in about half an hour; can you come back for me?'

'Certainly, Mr Oakman. Half an hour.' He climbed back into his cab and reversed before disappearing up the driveway.

Adam seemed puzzled as he watched the car out of sight. He shrugged his shoulders and moved to unlock the door of the carriage house.

Jessica walked into a living room of enormous proportions. The colours of autumn were everywhere. Huge overstuffed chairs of a dark rusty shade flanked a forest green sofa. The carpet was antique gold and the curtains a gold, green and brown plaid. Adam followed with their luggage.

'It's beautiful, Adam! Did your mother decorate this, too?'

He looked uncomfortable. 'Well, no. A—er—a friend did this. Come on, I'll show you around.' Jessica felt a stab of jealousy, but didn't ask any more questions as she followed him.

Behind the living room was a small kitchen with every conceivable modern convenience. A round oak table and two chairs with plump green cushions was centred in the curve of a bay window.

Jessica surveyed the scene outside through the glass. 'You'd never know how close to the city you are here. It's so quiet and beautiful, it's like being in the country.' She stood resting her fingers on a sill, studying a huge maple tree, bare of its leaves. 'Do you know that our house is less than three blocks from here?' So close, so very close, and yet so far.

'Yes, I knew that,' Adam said quietly. 'I've visited Dennis there many times. In the entrance hall hangs a portrait of you, sitting on a blue velvet chair.' He moved to stand behind her. She felt his hand feather over her hair lightly and blissfully closed her eyes.

'I was fascinated by that portrait,' Adam murmured. 'Your hair is like spun gold, and you look about twelve.'

'I was fourteen.' She sighed. 'Isn't it strange that we never met?' she said wistfully, turning to face him.

'Not strange at all, considering that you're ten years younger than I am. Do you want to see the rest of the house?' He spoke abruptly.

What did I say? thought Jessica as they re-entered the living room.

'When I did the remodelling I decided to keep this one big room rather than partition it. It has plenty of space for entertaining,' Adam explained, moving towards the staircase.

She followed him as he picked up the luggage and mounted the stairs to the bedrooms. He led her to a room at the front of the house which overlooked the gracefully curving drive, and deposited her suitcase on a luggage rack at the foot of the bed.

Jessica wandered over to open the yellow curtains and looked down on what must be, in the summer, a small but lovely rose garden.

'I'm sorry I have to go out for a while, Jess.

Why don't you rest? I'll be back to pick you up and we'll leave a few minutes before seven. The A.G. lives in the next block.'

'I . . . I'll be ready, Adam.' The hesitancy in her voice made him turn to her.

'What's wrong?' His tone demanded an answer.

'Nothing's wrong,' she spoke brightly. 'I'll just make myself a cup of tea, if you don't mind me puttering in your kitchen, and then rest.' She had her back to him and continued to gaze out of the window.

Adam turned her to face him. His hands were firm on her shoulders. 'Answer me!'

She lowered her head. 'Well, it just seems that we shouldn't be publicising this marriage so much if we're going to have it annulled.'

'If?'

'I meant "when",' she amended hurriedly.

'For my own reasons, I would like for us to act like any other newlywed couple,' Adam told her.

Her eyes flew to his.

'In public, of course,' he added. 'A little practice in private couldn't hurt, though.' As he spoke his lips covered hers in a brief warm kiss and he started to pull her closer.

Jessica arched away from him, afraid she would betray herself. 'You're forgetting the pact!' she reminded him nervously, averting her head.

'To hell with the pact! I need this.' His hand

tangled in the hair at the nape of her neck, bringing her face around to his.

She couldn't fight both her own weakness and the strength in those arms as they bound her to him. Slowly his mouth, lowered again until their lips were just touching. He murmured, 'You may never have learned to put out fires, but you sure as hell know how to start them!'

He pulled her on to her toes, his mouth bruising hers hungrily. One hand was at the base of her spine and the other circled to her back to crush her breasts against the hard wall of his chest. It was unavoidable that her lips opened under his and, as he explored them mercilessly, the kiss softened, became overwhelmingly sensuous.

Jessica obeyed the compelling command of his hands and lips and arched towards him. The flames ignited by their embrace threatened to consume them both, until the honk of a taxi horn brought them back to reality.

Adam reluctantly let her go, and her knees threatened to buckle as he stepped away. He raked unsteady fingers through his hair. He didn't touch her again, but his voice was husky as he said, 'While we're here, Jess, let's pretend we've just met. Washington's an exciting city, so let's forget the past twenty-four hours and enjoy ourselves.'

She looked at him. 'Can we forget?' she asked, her eyes troubled.

His mouth tightened and he frowned. 'We can try!' he said grimly. 'Let me do your worrying for you today, Jess,' he urged. 'Leave your mind free to concentrate on your husband for just a while.'

Her eyes widened in surprise.

'Please,' he added, and she nodded.

When he had left Jessica sank down on to the bed. Her thoughts were in a turmoil. Could she handle a brief affair with him? It was obvious that he wanted her, but her own feelings went much deeper than that. She wanted him too, but she wanted him for ever. If this were to be a brief last fling before he married another girl, she would be destroyed.

Still—a reckless gleam came into her eyes—why not enjoy these hours? They might be the only ones she would ever have. She consigned the faceless girl to the back of her mind with only a twinge of conscience and began to plan what she would wear tonight. Something that would knock Adam for a loop; she grinned at herself rashly.

When Adam returned at six-thirty, she was dressed and reading a magazine in the living room. He came in briskly and started towards the stairway, saying, 'I'll hurry, Jess. It took longer than . . .' His voice trailed off as he looked at her, stunned. He came to a stop, one foot on the bottom step.

'Well, well!' Slowly his eyes raked her, starting from the small foot in its high-heeled sandal up the curve of a well-formed calf, exposed by a slit in the black dress to the knee. His eyes continued up the fullness of her hips to the indentation of her tiny waist and over the full beauty of her breasts. There they paused, lingering on the curve that showed through another slit from the high neckline tied under her throat. He lifted his gaze to her face, now flaming, and up to her smooth blonde hair arranged in a sophisticated chignon. She had tucked a small silk rose into her hair and wore tiny jet earrings.

She tried to look at him calmly, but he was so dumbfounded that she couldn't suppress the hysterical giggle that rose in her throat.

The sound released him, and he moved. Crossing the room with long strides, he hauled her up against the length of his body.

She felt his muscular thighs through the thin material of the dress and her poise almost deserted her.

'You little devil! What are you declaring? War?' His hands restlessly caressed her bare arms, and he laughed at her shy blush. 'That blush doesn't go with the dress.'

Jessica was beginning to succumb to the effects of his smile. Her knees were weak, but she managed to answer calmly. 'I don't know what you're talking about. Hurry and dress, Adam, it's almost seven.'

'I doubt if anyone will notice what I'm wearing with you by my side, but I'll hurry.' He released her and headed for the stairway. Halfway up the stairs he paused again to look at her. She couldn't read his expression.

'I've seen you as my waif, my bride, and now my sexy siren. How many more of you are there in that lucious little body, I wonder?' he asked with amusement.

Jessica was astonished at the possessive note in his voice.

He was whistling as he disappeared. Whistling! She hoped she could cope with him in this mood. Well, she'd asked for it. She knew that she was a lot less sophisticated than she looked in this dress, and she hoped Adam realised it, too.

Tears welled in her eyes. If this weren't all a fantasy she could be so happy. If Dennis were safe, if her parents were home, if Adam weren't in love with someone else—if, if! Furiously she blinked to clear her vision.

When he returned a short time later his splendour matched her own. The gleaming white of his shirt front made his tan darker and he was staggeringly handsome in his black evening clothes.

Jessica was conscious of the width of his shoulders as he picked up her black velvet evening cape from the chair and held it open for her. She moved towards him. His hair was still damp from the shower and she could smell a slight scent of cologne on his freshly shaved cheeks as he put the cape around her shoulders.

Turning her to face him, he asked, 'Shall I call a cab?' He dubiously eyed her shoes.

'Not if it's in the next block. At least there's no snow on the ground.'

He pulled the fur-trimmed hood around her face. His knuckles touched her cheek gently. 'Are you sure you'll be warm enough?' he asked.

'I'm sure,' she said softly. There was a different atmosphere between them tonight, and she didn't want to disturb it. It was a mood of delicate tenderness that warmed her all the way to her toes. She could no more prevent her response to this masculine man than she could stop breathing.

His hands still held the edges of her hood. His eyes rested on her parted lips for a moment before he pulled them away. 'Let's go, then.'

Adam kept her arm firmly in his as they walked the short distance through the cold night.

A butler opened the door for them and took their wraps. Their host and his lovely wife entered the hall from a side door to greet them warmly. Introductions were made, and as the older woman offered her cheek for Adam to kiss, Jessica had a chance to study them both.

The Attorney-General was an imposing man. Tall, though not as tall as Adam, he had a thick shock of white hair over piercing green eyes. His wife's height almost matched his. The silver wings in her dark hair gave her an aloof, dramatic look. Jessica was slightly daunted until she met the gleaming merriment in the popping brown eyes.

Indicating the direction with a graceful hand,

she allowed Jessica to precede her into the drawing room.

They were not the only guests at the stately Georgian house. Jessica met a Senator and his wife from the West and a young couple, Sheila and Brad Logan, visiting from Boston.

Sheila was the niece of the Attorney-General's wife. She and Brad were taking their first vacation since the birth of a three-month-old daughter. Jessica sat next to her on a moiré love-seat, and Sheila chattered nervously about leaving the baby for the first time.

His boss had taken Adam off immediately they arrived, saying that they would get their business over with so they could relax and enjoy the rest of the evening.

Jessica liked Sheila. She was vivacious and talkative and was obviously very much in love with her husband. Her eyes followed him as he moved around the room to take orders and mix drinks.

'Can I get you ladies anything?' Brad asked them.

They decided on dry sherry and when he returned with their drinks, he laughed at Sheila. 'My dear, not everyone is as enamoured of our little Kitty as we are. Jessica may not be interested in hearing you extol her virtues.'

'I'm sorry, Jessica, I do get carried away, and I'm sure I'm boring you with my domestic chatter,' Sheila apologised.

'Oh, but I am interested! I love babies! I'd love a dozen,' Jessica laughed.

As she took her glass from Brad she looked up straight into Adam's eyes, which had darkened as he stood in the doorway watching her intensely.

Brad chuckled, 'Well, Adam, there you are! Your wife says she'd like a dozen children. How long have you been married? I think I heard two days.'

'Come and join us, Adam,' said Sheila, realising Jessica's embarrassment. She sent her husband a quelling look that bounced right off, and began to chat aimlessly about the weather.

Jessica avoided Adam's eyes, but she could not avoid the burning sensation she felt when his gaze rested on her.

Their hostess led them into the beautiful dining room. A fire burned cheerfully in the fireplace and the chandelier glimmered with a thousand prisms, reflecting on the shining silver and sparkling crystal.

Jessica was halfway through the creamy mushroom soup before she could garner the courage to look at Adam. When she did his eyes were alight with amusement.

She lifted her nose a quarter of an inch and turned to smile warmly at Brad, seated on her right. Adam thought it was funny, did he? She had only been trying to put Sheila at ease. He should have known that!

The Senator, on her left, engaged her in a

conversation she had to struggle to concentrate on.

Succulent roast beef and fresh tiny carrots were followed by a delicious strawberry mousse. Jessica was aware that Adam's glances were often on her as she spooned the confection into her mouth, but she ignored him.

Finally, dinner was over, and as they re-entered the parlour she left Adam's hand at her waist. She looked up at him over her shoulder.

'Twelve?' he jibed under his breath. 'We'd have to add on to the house!'

Her face flooded with colour. 'Adam, please!' she remonstrated.

'In that dress you're seductive enough, that I'd need very little encouragement.' His voice was low and only for her ears, but she looked around, fearful that someone had overheard. She twisted away from his hand and glared at him. He was certainly quick to take advantage of a situation. She wished she'd known that before she'd decided to wear this dress!

Numbly, she reached to take the coffee cup from her hostess and sank to the sofa beside her.

For the rest of the evening she was monopolised by the Attorney-General and his wife, who were casual friends of her parents and were anxious to hear news of them since her father's retirement. They were fascinated by her account of the sailing trip.

'What a wonderful idea!' her hostess said

wistfully. 'I wonder if we'll ever find the time to do all the things we've planned?'

Jessica felt a surge of compassion for the woman. They had uprooted their lives for an indefinite number of years because of something they believed in. It was an honourable position and an exciting life, but there were always the pressures, and the unconcealed life in a goldfish bowl. This cheerful woman would never complain, however.

Her husband's hand covered hers. 'Don't worry,' he said. 'We'll find the time.' He turned back to Jessica. 'I want to thank you, Jessica, for interrupting your honeymoon to fly up here.' He smiled. 'I wouldn't have blamed Adam if he'd consigned me to the devil, especially after meeting you, but it was necessary.'

'That's quite all right, sir, I understand, and you weren't interrupting . . .'

'Anything we haven't the rest of our lives for, haven't we, Jess?' Adam had walked to the back of the sofa, unnoticed, and he put a hand on her shoulder as he finished the sentence for her. 'If you'll excuse us, Jess and I had better be getting home.'

While he went for her coat, Jessica had a chance for a last goodbye.

She rose. 'It's been a lovely evening. Thank you.' She smiled at them both and spoke to each of the others in the room before joining Adam.

Her host accompanied her to the hall where

Adam waited. 'I'm sure we'll be seeing a lot more of you, Jessica. Adam is my right hand and I wouldn't be at all surprised to see him sitting in my chair some day.' Those green eyes twinkled. 'If he backs the right candidate, that is!'

As they descended the steps outside Jessica asked Adam, 'Would you want to be Attorney-General?'

'Wha-at? What makes you ask that? He wasn't serious, you know.'

He stopped under a street light to look at her in surprise, but she kept walking. 'Well, I just wondered. You seem to be different people, too.' She blushed, remembering their earlier conversation. 'I mean . . . well, at the beach you're different from the person you are here. You even look different!' She cocked her head and peered up at him.

Adam laughed. 'Which one do you like best?'

Both, she thought, but didn't answer his question. Instead she said, 'I think he was serious.'

He pondered for a moment. 'That's an interesting question, Jess. I guess, if I ever thought about it, that my time at Justice is temporary. When I got out of law school, I needed the experience. But when I think of my career, I think of practising law in Brunswick. That's really my home, and it's a restorative to me to go back. The sea breeze blows the cobwebs out of the brain and looking out at the vastness of the ocean keeps your thoughts in perspective and your priorities straight.'

Jessica mulled over his words. The longer she knew this man, the closer she felt to him and the more she respected the spirit of him. But part of his hypnotic appeal was the dynamic strength that flowed from him. She had first felt it when they met on the beach. Adam would be a good Attorney-General. The thought made her sad, for some reason.

They walked the rest of the way in silence. The night was dark but clear enough to see the stars twinkling overhead. Jess's hand was close in Adam's arm, his own covering it warmly.

As they entered the carriage house Adam said, 'Shall I make some coffee?' He took the cloak from her shoulders and hung it with his coat in the small closet by the front door.

'Don't you have to be up early?'

'Yes, but we can have one cup. That isn't what's going to keep me awake tonight,' he said mildly.

She whirled to stare at him. He lazily inspected her body in the black dress and casually walked towards her.

What was he expecting? Darn this dress! She hurried to the kitchen door. 'I'll make the coffee. You stay out here! And . . . and relax.'

'Fine,' he said as he shed his dinner jacket and began to pull at his tie.

Jessica dived through the door.

Her hands were unsteady as she filled the automatic coffee maker. She opened cabinets until she found a tray and cups and saucers. As the coffee perked she chastised herself for trying to be something she was not.

When she returned carrying the tray, she cast a brief look at him. The tie was gone and his shirt was unbuttoned halfway down, showing the dark springy hair on his chest. She caught her breath at his intense maleness.

His eyelids hid his expression. 'Put the tray here, Jess,' he said, indicating the table in front of where he was sitting on the sofa. She set it down and rubbed damp palms together.

'Aren't you going to pour me a cup?' His tones were still lazy.

Nervously she perched on the edge of the sofa beside him and reached for the pot of coffee, but her hand never made it.

Suddenly he grabbed her wrist and drew her back beside him. 'On second thoughts, let's forget the coffee,' he murmured. His arms went around her.

'Adam, there's something I have to tell you. It . . . it's about . . .'

'Shut up, Jess,' he growled, his lips at the sensitive spot below her ear.

Jessica was overpowered by his power and virility as his arms gathered her closer. She struggled to keep her head clear against the emotions which were taking charge.

'You're very provocative tonight,' he whispered just before his mouth moved to hers.

'But, Adam . . .' she wailed.

'I said shut up!' His lips, warm with desire, covered hers.

Her hands tangled in the hair on his chest, clinging, before she pushed hard and turned her head to avoid his kiss. 'Adam, you've got to listen to me!'

She gasped as he pulled the ribbon ties loose at the neckline of her dress, and his mouth found the curve of her breast. Closing her eyes to the exquisite sensations coursing through her body, she murmured his name softly.

'Do you know,' Adam muttered mildly as his warm lips on her stole her breath, 'that you have the most intriguing mole right here?' His tongue touched the spot. 'It's tantalised me all night. In this dress it's clearly visible, and I could hardly take my eyes off it.'

'This dress!' Her eyes flew open. 'Adam, this dress—it isn't me!' she cried desperately. 'My mother bought it for me, but even she didn't like it.'

He began to tremble under her hands, which had somehow got tangled in the hair at the back of his head.

'I'm not a sexy siren! I wanted to shock you. I'm sorry, Adam,' she cried.

As his hand began to caress her waist, his trembling grew stronger.

'Please, Adam,' she whispered.

'Please what?' he choked.

A premonition seized her. Her fingers tightened in his hair and she used it to lift his head. She stared unbelievingly. He was laughing! He was so choked with laughter that he couldn't speak. Laughing at her! All night she had searched her mind for a way to explain about the dress, and he had been enjoying her discomfort.

'You . . . you cad! You arrogant beast! Let me go!'

'Jess, I'm sorry. I just couldn't resist it.' Adam still held her, chuckling. 'When I came in tonight and saw you in that dress I was knocked flat for a minute. But you betrayed yourself with that giggle.' Then his voice deepened. 'You're still playing with fire, though. You know that, don't you?'

She began to struggle violently. 'Let me go!'

'O.K., in just a minute, but listen to me first.' The laughter had become that heartwarming smile and she fought its attraction. Her lips had begun to twitch, but she tightened them.

'I am not going to listen! I'm going to bed!' She gave a final push and was free and across the room before Adam could get to his feet.

But he had the last word anyway. 'Jess,' his husky voice followed her up the stairs, 'it doesn't matter what you have on,' he said, still amused. 'I'd still want to take it off!'

When she awoke the next morning it was late.

She showered hurriedly and dressed in a soft peach-coloured blouse and skirt and went downstairs. The house was quiet. Adam had gone, but there was a note in his bold black handwriting propped against the coffee-maker.

'Jess, the weather has closed in for the next twelve hours, but promises to be clear in the morning. We'll have to stay until then. I'll be back about six. We'll go to the Jockey Club for dinner, so get your glad-rags out.' She could imagine his amusement as he wrote that. The note was signed, 'Love, Adam. P.S. if you go out leave me a note!'

'Love, Adam.' Carefully she folded the note and slipped it into the pocket of her skirt. Like a lovesick teenager, she thought disgustedly, but she didn't throw it away.

After a quick breakfast of toast and coffee she called the taxi company, asking for Abe Allen, and went back upstairs for a warm jacket.

She descended the stairs with a note in her hand. 'Gone shopping. Love, Jess.' There, let him make of that what he would!

It wasn't snowing, but it was heavily overcast as Jessica stepped outside to meet the taxi.

Abe was smiling broadly. He held the door open for her. 'Good morning, Mrs Oakman. Where to?'

'I'm going to do some shopping in Alexandria, Abe.' She named the store.

As was the way with all Washington cab

drivers, Abe began to talk easily, and asked questions that from any other stranger would seem impertinent. But Washington was still a bit of a small town and long-time residents liked to keep up with news of each other.

Still Jessica was surprised at Abe's knowledge of her. He asked about her mother and father and even knew she had a brother! She was appropriately vague concerning Dennis, but she began to wonder about Abe.

They passed familiar landmarks and Jessica had a momentary pang of nostalgia. Washington would always be to her the world's most exciting city, but she preferred the more relaxed and casual life on the Georgia coast.

As he let her out on one of the cobblestoned side streets in Alexandria, Abe asked if he could call for her at any certain time.

'I don't know how long I'll be, Abe. Thanks anyway.' Jessica loved wandering the narrow streets and her favourite seafood restaurant was down by the waterfront. She would have lunch there.

Abe had deposited her in front of a small boutique. Before moving to Georgia, Jessica had worked here as a wardrobe planner. As she entered, the owner-designer, Mrs West, spied her.

Giving her a hug, she exclaimed, 'Jessica! We've missed you. Are you back in Washington for good?' Her welcome was warm and sincere.

'No, Mrs West, only for today; but I couldn't miss the chance to come in and say hello.'

'And look around a bit, hmm? Come upstairs. We really have missed you, Jessica. The new girl is showing promise, but so far she doesn't have your flair.' She talked non-stop as they mounted the steps and Jessica smiled to herself.

'Are you still taking design courses?' She frowned when Jessica shook her head. 'You mustn't give them up. So few people have your talent.'

'I've had to suspend them for a while,' Jessica told her. 'I was helping Mother and Daddy settle in, and a few other things have come up. I'm planning to resume this fall in Atlanta.'

'Ah, yes there are some excellent schools there. Look at this dress, Jessica. This smoky blue would be lovely with your eyes.'

The next two hours were spent trying on clothes and catching up on the news. When Jessica had made her final selections and was ready to leave, she thanked Mrs West sincerely. 'I've missed all of you. It's been so good being here.'

'We've missed you too, dear,' said Mrs West warmly. 'I'll send these things to the address you gave me. They should be there by four o'clock. Now, you must come back soon to see us, and let me know how you get along with those design courses.'

'I will, Mrs West, thank you. Goodbye.'

Leaving the shop, Jessica turned left towards the river. She suddenly felt very lonely. She wandered along aimlessly, barely glancing in the display windows until her attention was caught by the sign for an art gallery, new since she had been here. On impulse she went in and heard the tinkling of a bell somewhere in the rear of the building.

A tall thin young man appeared. 'Hello. May I help you?' He was obviously very nervous.

'I'd like to look around,' said Jessica. 'I used to work near here and noticed that your gallery is new.'

'Please feel free. I've been open for about a month. As you can see, I'm hardly covered up with customers,' he grinned.

'If these paintings are any example, I'm sure you soon will be!' Jessica answered wholeheartedly, looking around her. 'Are you the artist?'

'Yes. I'm Peter Vance.'

'I'm Jessica Gentry—Oakman.' Amending her statement quickly, Jessica realised that she hadn't told her former employer that she was married. Well, what difference did it make? She wouldn't be married for long, she thought regretfully.

She walked slowly through the gallery, her excitement growing. The paintings were small, glowing jewels. The light in them was so perfect that they seemed to be illuminated from within. Many of them were of the beach and ocean; there was something familiar about the settings.

'Isn't this the Georgia coast?' she asked, pausing in front of a painting of dunes dotted with graceful pawgrass.

'Yes, it is. I was in the Navy until a few months ago and was stationed in Jacksonville, Florida. I used to drive up there every weekend to paint. Do you know the area?'

'I live there now!' she said delightedly. 'You've captured it perfectly! I . . .'

Suddenly Jessica caught her breath. On the back wall was a painting, slightly larger than the others. It was also a beach scene, but the day was dark as though a storm would break at any moment. In this painting was a figure. The features were indistinguishable, but it was a man. His legs were apart, hands jammed into the pockets of khaki pants. He wore a navy blue windbreaker and his head was thrown back, the wind ruffling his black hair.

CHAPTER FIVE

JESSICA stared fascinated by the painting. Slowly she drew nearer. 'Adam,' she breathed softly.

'In the Garden of Eden? Hardly! He was on the beach one day when I was there. I was impressed with something about him.' I know what you mean, thought Jessica dryly. Peter continued, 'I seldom do figures but this one turned out well.'

'I'd like to buy this one,' she said. 'I must have it, Peter.' She had noticed an NFS, not for sale, tag on it. 'Please!'

'Well, I really hadn't planned to sell it right now. I'm getting ready for an exhibit. Perhaps later.'

'Oh, please, Peter,' she begged. 'I won't be back in Washington for a while and I want it so very badly. Please!'

Peter wasn't immune to those big blue eyes as she pleaded, and finally he relented. He named a figure that would just about empty her bank account, but she knew it didn't matter. She would always have this even when she no longer had Adam. She wrote out a cheque while Peter wrapped the picture securely in brown paper. She was so excited that she decided to skip lunch. Peter called her a taxi so that she could take the painting with her.

When the taxi came the driver was a stranger to her, and she was relieved. She didn't want to try to keep up with Abe's chatter when she was so excited over her new purchase.

Jessica could hardly sit still and, back at the carriage house she paid the driver hurriedly and took her prize upstairs, where she unwrapped it. She gazed at the figure. The storm clouds above him seemed to roll. This was the way she had first seen Adam, and this was the way she would always remember him.

Carefully she rewrapped the package and looked around. Taking her suitcase from the closet, she put it on the bed and opened it. She crossed her fingers. It fitted!

She didn't know what she would do with her clothes, but she couldn't let Adam see the painting. It might tell him things about her that she didn't want him to know.

Adam came in earlier than his note had said. He looked out of breath, but when he saw Jessica he seemed to relax visibly.

She had had a leisurely bath, but had decided to wear the smoky blue shirtwaister dress, so she was curled up on the sofa in a long white robe waiting for the delivery man to arrive from Mrs West's.

He loosened his tie and unbuttoned the top button of his shirt as he headed for the kitchen. Pausing in front of her, he smiled down. 'Hi. Did you have a good day?'

She answered his smile. 'Yes, did you?'

'Let me fix a drink and I'll tell you about it. Can I get you something?'

'Do you have dry sherry?'

'I think so.' He went into the kitchen to fill the ice bucket. When he returned his gaze was sharp as he handed her the sherry. He sank gratefully into a chair and propped his feet on the matching ottoman.

'Jess, our conversation last night was providential.'

'Which one?' she said wryly.

'The one about my career, naturally; which one did you think I meant?' He grinned before drinking deeply from his glass. 'The Attorney-General tried today to interest me in politics. He presented some pretty strong arguments, but I'd already been thinking about our conversation, and I've decided to leave Justice to go home and open a private law practice.'

'That's wonderful, Adam! I'm so happy for you!'

'I'm happy about it, too. It was a decision I would have made sooner or later, but circumstances make now the best time. I'll have several projects to finish up, but most of the work can be done from there and I can begin looking for an office.'

'Will you give up this place?' she asked.

'No, I'll keep it.'

'But why? Will you still be here often?'

'Probably not, but I prefer it to a hotel when I'm in town, and since I own it there's no need to give it up.'

'But I thought it went with the big house.' Jessica was surprised.

'It does. My grandmother left it to me, but I've always leased the big house,' Adam explained. 'This has plenty of room for me.'

'I should think so! If I remember it correctly from visiting Jeanine, it was huge! I can't imagine a bachelor rambling around in that!'

'I'm not a bachelor, Jess.'

The doorbell rang as he spoke and he went to answer it, giving Jessica time to quiet the heavy pounding of her pulse. Every time they seemed to be getting along well, he made some outrageous statement and she had to struggle to recover from it. From now on she would cease to be shocked at anything he said!

'Gentry?' She held her breath at his brittle tones. 'Yes, I'll sign for it.'

He came back into the room carrying her packages and put them down on a chair near the stairway. A cool mask had stolen over his features. 'A delivery for you.' His words were clipped, but he continued smoothly, 'What did you do today?' He was obviously irritated as he stood looking down at her, but she couldn't understand why.

Her tone was nonchalant as she told him about her visit to her former employer. Then she asked, 'Adam, what's wrong? Why are you annoyed?'

He looked at her steadily before answering. 'Jess, I told you I wanted this to look like a normal marriage. Why did you give Mrs West your name as Gentry?' His mouth had tightened, but Jessica breathed a sigh of relief ignoring his expression.

'Adam, I didn't give her my name at all, just the address. I forgot,' she said lightly.

'You forgot you were married?' he asked sceptically, sarcasm dripping from his tones.

'Yes, I did! I'm sorry, but I don't feel married!' She stood abruptly to face him.

A deathly silence followed her words and with wide eyes she watched Adam try to control his temper. Finally he said smoothly, 'Well, we'll have to see what we can do to change that.'

She hadn't meant to throw out a challenge and, half afraid, she took a step backward. Her knees were against the sofa, but Adam sat down again in the big chair.

He took a swallow of his drink and asked mildly, 'What's a wardrobe planner? I've never heard of one.'

Jessica swallowed hard and sank back on to the sofa. She tried to match his nonchalance. 'W-We kept detailed files of everything in a customer's wardrobe, plus sizes and colour preferences; then if she needs a suit for a political rally or a dinner guest for a fund-raising banquet we could make a selection for her. It's a big help for wives of politicians, and especially for women who are interested in politics themselves.' She still watched him warily as she explained further about her job. 'It saves them hours of trudging the streets to find the right shoes or accessories. Also we got to know them really well and could be sure that what we selected was something that they would like, and that would be suitable for them.'

'Like your dress last night?' His expression had softened and he was smiling again.

'Adam! I tried to explain . . .' her voice rose.

He got up from his chair and held out his hand. The uncomfortable moment had passed, it seemed. 'Okay, Jess—I was teasing. Now let's get dressed and we'll have dinner. Does the Jockey Club suit you?'

Jessica put her hand in his and was pulled easily to her feet smiling at him. 'Yes, I'm looking forward to it. I haven't been there since they remodelled the hotel and the food was always superb. Besides, I skipped lunch, and I'm ravenous!'

'Why did you skip lunch?' His hand tightened warmly on hers before releasing it.

She thought of the painting in her suitcase, but she couldn't mention that. 'Oh, I just wasn't hungry,' she replied vaguely.

The Fairfax Hotel on Embassy Row, one of Washington's oldest, had recently been completely remodelled. A white-gloved doorman helped Jessica from the car and opened the door to the small intimate lobby. The marble floor gleamed and they went up the few steps.

With Adam's hand at her waist they crossed the lobby to enter the Jockey Club. The cosy atmosphere and subdued lighting welcomed the seasoned traveller. Jessica's high heels clicked on highly polished, pegged hardwood floors as the maître d' led them to a red leather banquette. He slid the table out for them to sit beside each other.

'Mr. Oakman, good evening. You haven't been with us in some time.'

'No, John, I've been away. But I've looked forward to bringing my wife to sample your cheesecake.'

John discreetly nodded to Jessica, who realised that Adam was well known everywhere in this city. He must have quite a social life when he's in town, she thought, nettled. A prick of envy spurred her as she pictured the girls who must have shared his evenings . . . or more.

Their waiter brought menus and, when they declined cocktails, took their order.

Jessica looked around her. 'I'm so glad they didn't change the basic atmosphere when they remodelled. I like the sporting motif.'

'They have quite a collection of paintings. My favourite, Brooding Jockey by Ellis, is right above your head. Poor fellow, you can feel the defeat on his shoulders, can't you?'

Jessica twisted around to look behind her and up. When she lowered her eyes to smile her agreement to Adam, their faces were only inches apart.

He drew in his breath and the smile faded from her parted lips. They looked long at each other and the room receded around them. They were oblivious to the subdued clatter. It was as though they were in a vacuum.

'The Jockey Club would be properly shocked if I kissed you right now, wouldn't they?' Adam murmured huskily. His eyes searched her face tenderly, lingering on the moistness of her parted lips. He had taken her hand, interlacing their fingers tightly.

'We'd probably be thrown out on our ears,' she whispered through numb lips.

'Jess, I . . .' Whatever he had been about to say was interrupted by the waiter with their first course. A creamy, delicately flavoured soup was placed before them.

Gradually they returned to the world around them. Adam kept the conversation light during dinner, but between courses he held her hand firmly, his thumb occasionally touching the wedding band she wore.

They had just begun on the cheesecake when the maître d' approached their table. 'Mr Oakman, there's a telephone call for you in the lobby.'

'Excuse me, Jess—I'll be right back.'

When Adam returned to the table he said, 'We're going to have to leave right away. We're flying back tonight. Thank God, the weather's cleared.'

'Tonight, Adam? Has something happened? Is it Dennis?' Her voice shook.

'Dennis is fine—he was on the phone. Things are breaking quickly. It's all going as we planned, but I have to be on the scene.' He hurried her out through the hotel and into a waiting taxi.

Adam unlocked the door of the carriage house

and Jessica hurried upstairs to pack. She added what few clothes she could to the suitcase and stuffed the rest into her shopping bags. She changed into a yellow wool pants suit and was almost ready when Adam knocked on her door.

He picked up her suitcase with his and she followed carrying the shopping bags.

'What did you buy today? I'm not sure we can get the plane off the ground with this load,' he teased.

Jessica felt the blood rush to her face, remembering the painting. The frame was heavy!

Abe and his taxi were waiting to take them back to Washington National Airport. Everything was rushed until they finally settled into the little plane. Adam was busy with take-off, talking into his microphone, taxiing out, waiting for clearance from the tower.

'Abe was nice, wasn't he?' Jessica asked.

Adam chuckled. 'He works for the Department.'

'Wh-at? The Department of Justice?' she was dumbfounded. 'Why was he . . .?'

'Keeping an eye on you. You really threw him when you gave him the slip in Alexandria today. He called me, frantic. That's why I was home so early.'

'Do you think I'm really in danger, Adam?'

'Let's say I'm just not taking any chances,' Adam answered tersely, and returned his attention to the instruments.

When they were airborne he heaved a sigh. 'On our way! There's not much of a moon tonight. Why don't you crawl across to the back seat, Jess? There's a blanket back there and you can prop your feet up and sleep for a while.'

'In a minute. Aren't you sleepy, too? Will you be all right?'

'I'll be fine. You can pour me a cup of coffee from the thermos under your feet, but don't worry, I'll get you home safely.'

'I'm not worried, Adam,' she said softly. He threw her a penetrating glance. She poured coffee into the plastic cup and handed it to him.

Unbuckling her seat-belt, Jessica climbed into one of the back seats, curling up under the blanket. She slept deeply, undisturbed except for the occasional crackling of the radio, all the way back to the small St. Simon's Airport.

Jessica awoke at the slight jarring when the wheels touched down. 'Are we home already?' she asked drowsily.

'Yes, darling, we're home.' Adam's deep voice was gently soothing and she dozed again as he taxied to the hangar.

Strong hands lifted her out of the plane and strong arms carried her still wrapped in the blanket to the car. She gave herself up to the comfort of them, and drifted out of and into sleep as Adam drove to the rock and glass house.

Once, as he lifted her from the car, she opened her eyes, looked at the house, and smiled sleepily up at him. He smiled back and his arms tightened as he lowered his head to kiss her tenderly. She sighed, completely content.

When he had deposited her on the bed, he leaned over her, one hand on either side of her head and asked, 'Do you want me to undress you?'

'Yes, please,' she answered, still in a dream of her own.

His hands were gentle as he removed her shoes and her jacket. He unbuttoned her blouse, but when he raised her up to slide it off her eyes flew open. Her face was buried in his shirtfront. Her body stiffened.

'What do you think you're doing?' she demanded indignantly.

'I'm undressing you,' Adam said calmly as his hand went to the button of her slacks. 'You asked me to.'

She slapped furiously at his hand. 'I most certainly did not!'

He sighed. 'I was afraid it was too good to be true,' he said with mock seriousness. 'However, I'll have something for my trouble.'

Before she could stop him, he leaned over and softly kissed the mole just above the edge of lacy bra. He grinned down at her frowning face. 'Goodnight, Jess.'

The door closed behind him and Jessica blushed to the roots of her hair.

It had been after three when they landed, so

ten o'clock found her still burrowed under the covers, when the door was flung open.

'Wake up, sleepyhead! We're going sight-seeing!'

'Go away!' Jessica groaned from her warm nest. 'You're not serious?'

'Look at me and see how serious I am,' he laughed.

She raised her head slightly and opened one eye. Adam stood beside her bed with a tray in his hands. He was dressed in casual slacks and a red plaid shirt. The sleeves were turned back to reveal his strong forearms, lightly covered with hair. He grinned at her.

He looked so vigorous and masculine that she groaned again and buried her head before suddenly lifting it in surprise.

'Adam! Breakfast in bed!' She struggled to a sitting position, pulling the covers up under her arms.

'Just toast and coffee. We'll have lunch somewhere while we're out.' He set the tray across her lap.

Jessica lifted her fingers to run them through the tumbled glory of her hair. 'I've never had breakfast in bed when I wasn't sick before,' she said with delight, inhaling the rich aroma of the steaming coffee.

'It was the only way to get you moving. I looked in at you and you were dead to the world.'

'You looked at me when I was asleep?'

'Yes, and I'll admit I was tempted to crawl in with you. You looked very . . . cuddly.' His words trailed off.

Jessica glanced up at him in surprise at the unexpected huskiness in his voice and her mouth went dry.

His grey eyes darkened as they roamed over her. The covers had fallen away. Her pink nightgown was twisted and barely covered her breasts. One strap had fallen off her shoulder. She reached quickly for the sheet, but Adam forestalled her.

His gaze was devouring and his hand trembled slightly as he slipped the strap back on to her shoulder, then covered her with the sheet.

Emotion overwhelmed her and kept her speechless. He leaned down to kiss her parted lips slowly and thoroughly. 'Do you see, now, why we're going sightseeing?' he said against her mouth.

She nodded and lowered her lashes to hide the expression in her eyes from him. 'Adam, what are we going to do?' she asked huskily. Her fingers gripped each other in her lap. How much longer could she take this?

He lifted her chin. 'Trust me, Jess.'

'I do, but . . . but . . .'

He tasted the sweetness of her lips once more before he straightened. 'I'll give you twenty minutes!'

Jessica was ready in fifteen. Dressed in the

same yellow pants suit she had worn last night, she went into the living room. 'It's a beautiful day for sightseeing,' she said. She was determined to hide her vulnerability, though she still trembled from his kisses.

'Dennis called again this morning,' Adam told her as they were driving over the causeway towards Brunswick. 'He expects things to be quiet today, but I'll pick up a paging beeper in Brunswick to keep us in touch.'

'Did . . . did he say when he'd be back?' Jessica had been very quiet during the trip and her voice was still hesitant.

'It won't be long, Jess.'

As soon as they came off the causeway Adam pulled into a shopping centre and went into an electronics store. He returned with the paging device and they were quickly on their way again.

'I thought we'd start at Jekyll Island. Have you been there?' he asked.

'No, I haven't. Isn't that where the Millionaires' Club was located?'

'That's right. How much do you know about it?'

'Not much, only that a group of wealthy men built homes there.'

'Astor, Morgan, Carnegie, Pulitzer, Rockefeller, to name just a few. And it was the fear of death that sent them to Jekyll Island. They sent two doctors from Johns Hopkins to search the world for a spa which would be the healthiest possible place, have natural beauty, good water, semi-tropical climate, and isolation. The scouts combed the earth, from the French Riviera and the southern coast of the Mediterranean to California, and finally recommended the Golden Isles of Georgia.

'There were one hundred members of what was called "the world's most exclusive club" and they represented one-sixth of all the world's wealth.'

As Adam talked the tension between them eased and Jessica began to enjoy herself unguardedly. 'One-sixth! My goodness!'

'Yes! But today Jekyll is owned by the state of Georgia, and the whole island is a state park and popular convention centre. There are tourists here the year round.'

When they reached the island Adam turned left off the divided highway on to a side road. He parked the car in front of a large gingerbread Victorian house surrounded by acres of park. 'This was the Rockefeller "cottage" and it's now the island museum.' He came around to help Jessica from the car. As they walked to the museum he took her hand, and explained, 'None of the original cottages had complete kitchens. The hotel, where we'll go next, was staffed by the finest chefs from Delmonico's in New York City. Most of their meals were eaten there.'

The hostess on duty welcomed them, and gave them a guide book. With twinkling eyes she said to Jessica, 'Be sure to sit in the Chinese Wishing Chair. All our honeymooners like to do that!'

Jessica gasped. 'But we're . . .'

'Here for that very reason,' Adam interrupted, and took her arm firmly.

The girl laughed. When they were out of earshot Jessica hissed at him, 'How did she know? And why did you say that?'

He shrugged. 'Don't you want us to have a happy marriage . . . however long it lasts?'

She couldn't think of a reply, so she flipped through the guide book in seeming unconcern. She soon found herself fascinated by the museum with its beautiful stained glass and priceless furniture. As they roamed through she besieged Adam with questions.

Finally they came to the room where sat the heavily carved ebony Wishing Chair. Jessica looked at it doubtfully, but Adam resolutely settled her on the hard wooden seat. She was penned in by his bulk. He leaned over her, his hands on the arms of the chair.

'Now, close your eyes and wish,' he needled. 'Come on, Jess. We need all the good luck we can get,' he urged, smiling.

She looked up at him and closed her eyes. I wish . . . oh, I wish Adam loved me as much as I love him, she thought. She heard him murmur her name before his lips touched hers. Unbidden, her arms circled his neck.

Adam's arms went around her and he lifted her

out of the chair, deepening the kiss. When he raised his head, she opened her eyes to see an expression in his that she had never seen there before. For an unguarded moment there were no barriers between them. She could almost believe that her wish had been granted. Almost . . .

Then Adam released her and turned away, pushing his hands into his pockets. A noisy group of people entered behind them. Without saying a word they moved to the next room.

By the time they finished their tour Adam had again taken her hand.

'Let's go to see the hotel, Adam. Is it far? Can we walk?'

He grinned down at her. 'We could, but let's take the car and then we can make a circle of the island for you to see some of the other cottages. The others are only opened for special occasions, but I think you would enjoy driving by.'

They stopped at the old rambling pink and white hotel and Adam took her into the library to see the guest book with its famous last entry, General George S. Patton.

He explained, 'A German submarine was sighted off the coast of Jekyll in the spring of 1942. President Roosevelt was concerned because the men vacationing here represented most of the financial might of the country. So he dispatched General Patton, pearl-handled revolvers on his hip, to close the club.'

'It's fascinating!' Jessica enthused as they left

the hotel across the wide veranda. 'But will you tell me why there's a Canadian flag flying here?'

'Because so many visitors from Canada come down during the winter. Every year the Jekyll Island Authority flies their flag as a sign of welcome.'

When they had finished their circle of the island Adam announced, 'It's time to find some lunch.'

CHAPTER SIX

ADAM headed the car back over the causeway to Brunswick and then on towards St Simon's Island. About halfway over they stopped at a lovely restaurant right on the marsh. Sitting by a large picture window, they watched a family of rabbits foraging in the tall marsh grass. From their table they could see not only the rabbits but marsh hens and gulls feeding in the fertile grasses.

The restaurant was beside the inland waterway marina. They finished lunch, and as they were leaving, Adam pointed out his sailboat moored there.

'I didn't know you sailed.' Jessica smiled up at him and he rested his arm lightly across her shoulders.

'If you grew up on this coast a boat was as important to you as a car. My first one was a rowboat. Later, a speedboat was the only thing that would satisfy me. It wasn't until I was about eighteen that I began to appreciate the advantages of sailing. Would you like to go aboard?'

'I'd love to. Dennis taught me to sail young. He didn't tolerate fools easily, so I'm a fairly good crew.'

'Good! We'll take her out one of these days and I'll see how well he taught you. There are some beautiful places around here that you can't reach by car.'

'One of these days.' Jessica pondered his words. She felt what was becoming a familiar ache in the pit of her stomach.

They walked hand in hand across the docks to the boat. Sleek and white, it was larger than it had looked from the restaurant.

'Adam! She's a beauty! How long is she?'

'Seventy-five feet. I bought her five years ago. Until then I had a small sloop, but I decided that I wanted to travel further, take a trip to the Bahamas, and maybe Mexico, so I got this yawl. So far I haven't had time for a single trip,' he said dryly.

As Adam took her arm to help her aboard, a voice hailed him from the next slip.

'Frank—good to see you! Come aboard!' Adam grinned at the rotund man in faded jeans who jumped across the narrow expanse of water and on to the deck. They shook hands eagerly.

Adam put out an arm and pulled Jessica in to rest against the length of him. 'Frank, I want to introduce you to my wife, Jessica. Jess, this is Frank Newsome. We grew up together.'

Frank grabbed her hand. 'Your wife? Adam, this is great! I'm glad to meet you, Jessica, really glad!'

'Your enthusiasm is gratifying,' Adam laughed. 'But why are you here in the middle of the week? Don't tell me the brokerage business is that bad, or good?'

Frank was still grinning at Jessica with delight. He answered Adam absentmindedly, 'What? Oh, no, it rides along. I'm meeting a client here later. This is great!' he repeated.

Jessica laughed. 'So is this! I've never been greeted so charmingly before!'

Frank turned to Adam. 'I'm really glad you came to your senses, old buddy. All your friends were afraid Vanessa had got her hooks into you.' He clapped Adam on the back.

The arm around her shoulders tightened and Jessica looked up to find him frowning.

Vanessa—so that was her name! Jessica disengaged herself, and turned away pretending to study the rigging as the men continued their conversation. The blood was pounding in her ears and tears burned behind her eyelids. Hands clenched into fists, she walked on stiff legs to the bow. How long she stood there looking out over the marshes she didn't know. She loved Adam so much! How was she ever going to survive after this was all over?

She heard her name and turned to wave to Frank, who was back on his own boat.

'Do you want to see below?' Adam called.

Nodding, she made her way back to him, and they descended the few steps to the main cabin.

Jessica was quiet, only speaking to give the required responses as Adam showed her the galley and sleeping quarters. After locking up Adam jumped lightly to the dock and reached back to give her a hand.

Back in the car he looked at her speculatively. 'You're very glum all of a sudden. Aren't you having a good time?'

She swallowed the tears at the back of her throat and answered gaily, 'Yes, I'm having a wonderful time! Where are we going next?'

He studied her further before answering, 'I'm taking you to Fort Fredrica. It was one of the remote outposts of the English troops who were battling the Spanish for control of the south-eastern part of the country. It was abandoned in the middle 1700s. Time and nature have taken their toll and there's very little of the fort left, but to me it's the most beautiful spot on the island.'

Adam turned left and followed a narrowing road.

'Who's Vanessa?' Jessica blurted suddenly.

He laughed. 'Is that what's bothering you?' His

tones were caressing as he added, 'Are you jealous, Jess?'

'Certainly not! Why should I be jealous? This marriage doesn't mean anything. I just wondered. Is she . . .' She couldn't finish.

Adam's hands clenched on the wheel. He turned the car sharply into the parking area which was almost deserted and swung into a space near the gate before he answered curtly, 'Forget Vanessa!'

'Forget her? How can I forget her? Look what I've done to her!' she cried.

'Jess, my feelings toward Vanessa haven't changed, so there's nothing to blame yourself for. Why don't we just relax and see what happens.'

She reached numbly for the doorhandle.

They got out of the car and walked along the paths through what had been a bustling town centuries ago. Now there were only the outlines of foundations to show where houses and shops had been. Jessica felt a heavy weight in her heart. She lifted her chin with a determined movement; the burden would have to be endured, the days lived through, one at a time. Adam, whose shoulders were broad enough for anything, bore the heavier load and she wouldn't, couldn't add to it.

He took her hand, raising it to his lips briefly before intertwining his fingers with hers. 'Forget Vanessa,' he said again, gently this time.

She was surprised at his affectionate gesture and as he started to explain about the fort, she listened with only half an ear. 'Forget Vanessa', he had said. Well, she would!

She should loathe herself for taking this risk, but she couldn't. The joy of being with him, even though it could never be permanent, and even in such appalling circumstances, couldn't be denied. Maybe it was a reckless thing to do, but she would forget Vanessa for today! Taking a deep breath she smiled up at him. 'This is the most peaceful, quiet place I've ever seen,' she said. The branches of the trees almost grew to form a tunnel, but looking straight up there was clear blue sky. Festooned with Spanish moss, some of the live-oak trees were forty feet tall, and hundreds of years old. The tranquility of the scene calmed Jessica's anxiety.

They ambled hand in hand towards a point of land where sat the only remaining structure of the old fort. Adam led her to a piece of rock and sat down, pulling her with him. For a while they were silent, looking out over the inland waterway. Everything was still, as though nature held her breath.

It felt so natural that she didn't know when it had happened, but Adam's arm was around her, her head resting on his shoulder. She tilted her head to look up at him. His eyes were on her face. She tried to quell a rush of feeling and unconsciously licked her dry lips.

'That was as bold an invitation as I've ever had, Beachcomber!' he chuckled.

'What was?' she asked breathlessly.

His tongue intimately followed the path hers had taken. 'That! But we don't want to put on a show for the class of schoolchildren coming towards us, do we?'

Her face flamed as she drew away from him and turned to see a group of about twenty, nine- or ten-year-olds, shepherded by three harassed teachers.

'Let's go.' Adam's voice was husky. 'I want to get you alone someplace where I can kiss you thoroughly, the way I've wanted to ever since we were in the Jockey Club last night.' As they rose he kept his arm firmly around her shoulders and she slipped hers around his waist. His voice was mesmerising her as he said in her ear, 'We always seem to be either surrounded by people or too near a bed for your peace of mind.'

Jessica's eyes widened and she swallowed. 'I didn't think you'd noticed—about the bed, I mean.'

He laughed. 'Except for our wedding night, you've been as nervous as a cat every time I touch you.' His voice deepened. 'But that night I could have made love to you, couldn't I, Jess?'

She couldn't speak. She dropped her head, but he immediately raised it with a finger under her chin. 'Don't be frightened, sweetheart. I'm not going to take you to bed, not yet.' His lips feathered her cheek.

They had arrived at the car, and as she got in he asked, 'No comment?' She shook her head.

No comment, but inside she cried bitter tears of frustration. Would she be able to resist him? Could she conquer her own desire?

Adam drove south for a short distance and pulled into a side road which led to the bank of a river. Seldom used, the dirt surface was only slightly wider than a path.

'This is Ebo Landing, where illicit slave trading was carried on after 1798 when Georgia outlawed the trading of African slaves.' He parked the car at the end of the lane facing the river. 'It's a quiet place now when you think of the horror of what happened here.'

Everything was still except for the lazy movement of the water. The banks were lined with scrub palmetto. Across the river Jessica could see a huge live oak tree, its limbs covered with dripping moss, 'the bearded oaks', they were called. Slowly the bird calls resumed.

Jessica looked at Adam and saw that he had been watching her. She knew that the love was shining in her eyes and she didn't care. She smiled tremulously at him.

'Come here,' he said gruffly, lifting her easily over to cradle her on his lap. His eyes searched her face as he released the fastener at the nape of her neck to free her hair. His fingers laced through the length of it. Her scalp tingled at the warmth of his touch and her heart began to pound at the look in his eyes.

'Your hair is like sunshine,' he said huskily as he lifted a strand to his lips. His fingers traced her features with a soft touch. Smoothing the hair back, he outlined her ear and down her neck until he came to the collar of her blouse. He followed the edge to the buttons.

She caught her breath as he loosened them one by one until her lacy bra was exposed.

'Adam, no!' She pushed at his hands. 'We can't!' Waves of sensation threatened to drown her, but she fought to surface, gasping for breath. She tried desperately to turn her thoughts to Dennis, his danger, to Vanessa's place in Adam's life, but she found herself succumbing to his nearness. His touch was bringing every nerve end to stinging life.

Adam smiled, but his eyes followed his fingers, touching lightly as they travelled the border of lace and outlined the full curve of her breast. They seemed to have a life of their own, as they slipped inside the lacy cup. She gasped as they sought and discovered a hardening nipple. 'Please, no!' she choked.

He ignored her protest and lowered his lips to the tiny mole.

Jessica felt her will drain away, her feelings rushing in to fill the void. She leaned her head back to expose her throat to his tantalising exploration. She gave herself up to the fire he had ignited, that was threatening again to engulf her.

The buttons of his shirt were open and her feverish hands moved over his chest and up, around his neck, and into the thick springy hair at the back of his head.

He looked down into her upturned face. Her eyes were half closed with passion. His own were darkening rapidly. Slowly he allowed her to pull his head down, but he buried his face in her neck, still not giving her the fulfilment of his lips.

She gave a little groan of frustration deep in her throat. 'Adam, what are you doing to me?' she whispered.

He lifted his head. The sensual curve of his mouth mocked her. 'The same thing you did to me when you wore that sexy black dress, you little vamp! How do you like it?' Then his lips were subduing her protest, crushing hers; tasting, then devouring, as though he would never have enough of them. The hand which had tormented her so became hard as it went to her hip, forcing her closer to him.

Jessica's arms tightened. He was kissing her eyes, cheeks, the tip of her nose. His lips were restless on her face. She murmured his name over and over. She returned the kisses, choked by the fullness in her heart.

Suddenly Adam lifted his head. His eyes were blazing, his breathing laboured, and he was fighting for control. He opened the door of the car and got out, taking her with him roughly. 'We'd better walk,' he groaned as he set her on her feet, and rammed his hands into his pockets, turning away.

But her feet wouldn't move. She reached out, with hands behind her for the car, to keep from falling.

Adam took a step and looked back over his shoulder. He stopped and turned to face her. He rasped, 'God, Jess!' His hand came out in a pleading gesture. 'Don't look at me like that! I promised Dennis ...' He broke off, and then dropping his hand he was reaching for her.

Unconsciously she lifted her arms and the movement brought her body against the length of him in total surrender.

His hands were at her hips, straining her to him. When he felt her capitulation he seemed to abandon all control. 'I want you, Jess. God, I want you!' he murmured, and the fervid desire in his kiss branded her for all time as his.

He raised her high in his grasp and buried his lips in the hollow between her breasts. 'Hell, who needs a bed?' he growled as he swept her up in his arms and carried her to the grassy bank beside the river. He laid her gently on the ground and lowered himself beside her.

His caresses were slow now, and patient, but as his mouth moved again to her parted lips, her hands on his chest felt the racing of his heart, echoing her own.

All at once he groaned and rolled away from her. 'Damn! Damn!' The words erupted explosively from him. And then she heard it, too, the steady signal from the paging device on the front seat. Adam got to his feet and strode to the car, flicking off the pager. He sighed, but his breathing was still irregular as he said, 'Let's go! I've got to get to a phone!'

'Yes.' As she tried to rise she almost stumbled and Adam was there to help her up. She started to button her blouse, but her fingers didn't work very fast. Roughly he pushed her hands aside and did it for her.

Jessica was confused. He seemed to be angry. She looked up at him as he helped her into the car.

He grabbed her shoulders and shook her. 'Dammit, Jess, I've had about all I can take! Don't look at me like that again!'

'Adam, what's wrong with you?' She was almost in tears.

'You know what's wrong! Unless you're a hell of a lot more naive than you look!'

She subsided in her seat, without saying anything more. But her emotions were in a turmoil.

How could she have surrendered to him so completely? she asked herself despairingly. If the interruption hadn't come . . . She turned to stare blindly out the window, tears stinging her eyes. Shame was like a huge lump in her throat. Adam didn't love her. He wanted her—that was indisputable—but he was in love with someone else and his feelings hadn't changed.

He backed the car down the lane to the road. Heading back to the main part of the island, Adam stopped at the first telephone booth.

Jessica watched him through the glass of the cubicle. His hair was disordered and strain had deepened the lines around his mouth. He ran a hand across his forehead while he talked to someone on the other end of the line.

Finally he hung up. Getting back into the car, he said, 'I have to meet someone in Brunswick in an hour. I'll take you home first.'

Jessica nodded, but didn't trust herself to speak until they pulled into the driveway. 'Can I fix you something to eat before you go, Adam?' she said quietly.

'You can fill the thermos with coffee while I take a shower. A cold one!'

She didn't answer. When they got inside she headed to the kitchen as he went to the back of the house.

When she had started the coffee, she decided to make him a ham sandwich. If he didn't have time to eat it he could take it with him.

As she was filling the thermos he walked into the kitchen, wearing black jeans and a black turtleneck sweater. His hair was damp. Her knees weakened at the sight of his masculine potency, but she said calmly, 'I fixed you a sandwich. Do you have time to eat it here or shall I wrap it in foil?'

'Quite the concerned little housewife, aren't you?' he said sarcastically. 'Wrap it up.'

'Don't take your bad temper out on me! It wasn't my fault!' she reproached.

He was beside her, grabbing a handful of her hair to force her head back. 'That's right, it wasn't your fault. You were more than willing, weren't you, Jess?' he said silkily.

Jessica tried unsuccessfully to ease the pressure on her hair. 'Not any more, I'm not! Let go of me!' she spat angrily, but already tears were shimmering in her eyes.

'Just remember this!' he growled against her lips. 'I still want you, and I intend to have you!' His mouth came down bruisingly. 'Don't forget where we left off!'

Jessica pushed against him, and when he let her go, she ran to the bedroom and slammed the door. She leaned back on it, her body shaking violently. How could he be so cruel?

She took a shower, standing for a long time beneath the stinging spray. Slowly the anger inside her began to ease, to be replaced by a heavy sadness. She could understand Adam's behaviour. She had wanted him to make love to her and hadn't even tried to hide the fact from him. Her face flooded with colour when she realised that Adam had been fighting for control for both of them. He had promised Dennis to take care of her until this was all over. And he probably had made some promises to Vanessa, too. Humiliation at her behaviour swept through her.

Adam didn't want to leave any scars, and he was right! It was going to be hard enough to live with the knowledge of her love for him.

Stepping out of the shower, she wrapped herself in the terrycloth robe and, padding into the kitchen on bare feet, fixed a sandwich and poured a glass of milk. She stood looking out at the ocean as she ate.

Where was Dennis tonight? Adam had said that things were beginning to break. The tension which was building in him was obvious. Would all this be over by dawn, or maybe tomorrow? 'God, please keep them both safe,' she whispered, raising her eyes to the heavens. And help me to remember that Dennis is my only reason for being here with Adam, she added silently.

Propped up in bed later with a book, she tried to keep her attention on what she was reading, but it was impossible. Finally she turned out the light. Her tossing and turning ended hours later. When she heard Adam come in, she rolled on to her side and immediately fell asleep, but her sleep was restless. Twice during the early hours she got out of bed to splash cold water on her flushed face, and she was grateful when the night was over.

CHAPTER SEVEN

JESSICA stood at the window looking out at a bright, beautiful day. What a shame that her mood didn't match the sunshine. Yesterday had started out so well, she mused. When she had sat in the Wishing Chair, it had almost seemed as though its promise would be fulfilled. She loved Adam so much that she was ready to give herself wholeheartedly to him on the river bank. But then he had changed. Her frustration was magnified in him a hundred times, and he apparently blamed her.

She sighed deeply and went to the closet. Emerging from the bathroom fifteen minutes later, she looked up to see Adam coming through the door. All she wore was a towel loosely draped around her, and she took an automatic step backwards. His maleness seemed to fill the room and it was hard to breathe. He wore a brown tweedy sweater which fitted closely to the muscles of his arms and chest; strong thighs and lean hips were emphasized by well-fitting jeans.

He stopped, his fists clenched, when he caught sight of her. 'I did knock.' His gaze smouldered over her, lingering on the smoothness of her shoulders and the damp tendrils curling at her neck.

'I was in the shower,' Jessica said unnecessarily. 'I didn't hear you.' Her voice wobbled. She knew she was well covered in the huge towel, but at the look in his eyes which mentally stripped her, her mouth went dry. Her bare toes curled into the carpet to fight an urge to retreat into the bathroom.

Finally his eyes lifted to hers. His voice was hoarse. 'I have to go out again, Jess. I'll be back before lunch.' Still he didn't leave.

'The rest of the typing will keep me busy.' She tried for lightness. 'See you later, Adam.' She didn't want to stir his anger to a repeat of yesterday's sarcasm.

'Yes, see you later.' He turned to go, but at the door he stopped, his fingers white as he gripped the knob. 'I almost forgot—there's a midwinter dance at the club tonight. I should be there, as I'm on the board. Is that all right with you?'

Her eyes widened. 'I was supposed to go with Kevin—I'll have to call him.'

'Sorry to break up your date!' he said sarcastically, and left.

As she dressed in a blue Oxford-cloth blouse and tan slacks, Jessica's eyes were thoughtful. She had been right: he was two different men. In Washington he was smooth, civilised, controlled. He acted as though she were playfully amusing, and she had been fascinated by his urbane manner. He had teased her, laughed at her, and been warmly affectionate.

Here, at the beach, he was totally different. Here his sensuality was a tangible thing. He was barely controlled. His eyes raked her, smouldered when he looked at her, and his voice was husky or harsh when he spoke. Here, she was a little frightened of him. And yet it was impossible for her not to respond to his masculinity. But he was like a stick of dynamite, lit, and ready to explode, and she must forestall that explosion or be destroyed by it.

Jessica slipped on a pair of tan leather boat shoes and started out of the room. She hesitated, then turned back to the dressing table. Dividing her hair into three fat sections, she began to braid it.

In the kitchen she poured herself a cup of coffee and stepped through the glass doors on to the deck. The early morning chill soon sent her back inside, however, and with a sigh she went to the living room and approached the desk.

She set her coffee cup down. But the typing could wait for just a little longer! Turning her back, she quickly crossed to the hall and went down the length of it, to the room Adam had come out of that first day. Hand on the knob, she paused, then opened the door.

Stepping across the threshold, Jessica gasped with pleasure at the sight that met her eyes. It was like being out of doors. Two walls were of glass, one giving an angled view of the sea and the other, looking out over dunes dotted with sawgrass plumes. A huge bed dominated the room. It was covered in a textured woven spread of a sand colour.

In one corner were a pair of comfortable armchairs upholstered in grass green corduroy. Bookshelves lined an entire section of wall, floor to ceiling. Jessica was drawn to them. Running a finger over the titles on one shelf, she was fascinated by the variety of subjects Adam seemed to take an interest in.

Suddenly the finger stopped. Resting on the shelf, facing down, was a picture frame. With a sense of dread Jessica slowly picked it up. When she turned it over she was disconcerted by the sultry gaze of the girl looking out at her.

It was a dramatic portrait, in black and white. The lighting was from one side only which threw half of the picture into deep shadow, but the other half of that face was ravishing.

Dark hair framed a high forehead and prominent cheekbones. The eyes, edged by thick lashes, were large and sleepy-looking and the glistening mouth was an invitation to kiss. This must be Vanessa!

Jessica's shoulders slumped. The sophistication of this woman . . . you couldn't possibly call her a girl . . . would be a perfect complement for Adam's impressive good looks. Her imagination could almost see the two of them together. Was she short or tall? What colour were her eyes? It was impossible to tell from the photograph. Slowly she replaced it in it's original position and turned away dejectedly.

Jessica crossed the thick carpet of a slightly darker sand shade and looked down at the bed. Tentatively she sat on the edge. As she ran her hand over the fabric she wondered why she was torturing herself like this. The bed was neatly made, but she reached up and pulled out one of the pillows from under the spread. She buried her face in it, revelling in the clean masculine smell. A tear fell on to it as she lifted her face. Resolutely she replaced the pillow and smoothed the material back over it, then quickly left the room, closing the door behind her.

Back at the desk she took a sip of tepid coffee and rolled a piece of paper into the typewriter. Forcing her concentration on the lists of figures, she worked steadily until it was time for lunch.

She was heating a hearty bean soup when she remembered that she hadn't called Kevin. His secretary was properly evasive until she gave her name, Jessica Gentry Oakman. There was a long interval before Kevin came on the line.

'Jessica? Is that you?'

'Yes, Kevin.'

'What in the world is this Oakman business?' He sounded irritated.

'Well, I—er—I've got married, Kevin,' she answered shakily.

'Married!' He was shocked, and she smiled to herself. 'To Adam Oakman? I didn't even know you knew him! When did this happen?'

Jessica evaded, 'You didn't? Well—er—he and my brother have been friends for years!'

'It certainly was quick, wasn't it?' He was becoming sarcastic, and Jessica didn't appreciate his churlish attitude. She responded with haughtiness.

'We saw no reason to wait. Anyway, I won't be attending the dance with you tonight.'

'Of course,' Kevin laughed unpleasantly. 'I don't usually date married women. Will we see the two of you there?'

'I believe Adam plans for us to come,' she said, her hand gripping the phone tightly.

'Good! We'll see you tonight!'

As she hung up the phone Jessica wondered about the 'we'. She had never heard Kevin use the royal 'we' before, but if not, who did he mean? He had planned to take her and, obviously, intended to make a party of it.

Jessica heard the front door open and hurried to make a salad to serve with the soup, which was now bubbling away.

Quickly she tore lettuce into bite-sized pieces and added mushrooms, chopped earlier, and crumbled crisp bacon on the top. She tossed it all with a light Italian dressing, and was dividing it into two wooden salad bowls when Adam came into the room.

'Hi,' he said impassively.

'Hi,' she answered. 'Lunch is ready.'

Jessica risked a peep at him. There was a black scowl on his face, but he didn't look worried as he took his place at the table. She had already set two places at the table in front of the window.

Lunch was mostly a silent affair and, as they ate, Jessica felt her nervousness returning. She finished hurriedly and was already putting dishes into the dishwasher before Adam was through eating.

She went back out to the desk and Adam followed, settling on the sofa to work. He reached for a book, but before opening it he said, 'Will you please unbraid that ridiculous pigtail? It makes you look like a child!'

Jessica looked at him in stupefaction.

His eyes were cold and uncompromising. He lowered them to the book, but still she didn't move. 'Take it down!' he repeated angrily.

With shaking fingers she pulled the hair loose. Tears welled in her eyes and despite herself, she sniffed.

He glanced up but didn't say anything.

As the afternoon shadows lengthened Jessica broke the silence that had descended. 'Adam, I'm on the last page. Are there any more after these?'

'There are about four more pages. I'll have them for you in a minute.' Adam came over to stand behind her chair. He leaned over her shoulder to pick up a page of her typing. She could feel his warm breath on her neck and had to steel herself not to shrink from his nearness.

He hesitated before saying, 'These are beautifully done, Jess. Thank you.' Moving back to the sofa, he caught her eyes on him. She dropped them hurriedly to the typing in front of her.

An hour later Jessica finally lifted her fingers from the keys and flexed them. She stood up and stretched her back, tired from the unaccustomed sitting for so long. She glanced at Adam and stood stock still. His eyes were riveted on her breasts, their fullness outlined against the blue material as she stretched. She turned away, blushing.

'I need a break. Would you like some coffee, Adam?' She tried to keep her voice steady.

'We both need a break,' he said grimly. 'How about a walk on the beach?'

'Fine,' she answered. 'The fresh air will do us good.'

Adam took two windbreakers, a blue and a yellow one, from the coat tree beside the door. 'It will be too big, but you can push the sleeves up,' he said, helping her into the blue jacket. 'And there's a hood in the collar, in case it's too windy for you.'

The wind was strong as they crossed the dunes, but Jessica welcomed the fierceness of it on her face. They walked slowly along the edge of the ocean, letting the tension drain from them.

Jessica inhaled the freshness of the salt air and

gave a deep sigh. She decided to try to lighten the atmosphere between them. 'I love this place,' she said. 'When Mother and Daddy decided to retire here I'd only been down once, but I loved it. It's such a beautiful area, with the marshes on one side, the sea on the other, and the abundance of wildlife. I wish they hadn't sold their boat when they left Washington. I'd like to explore some of the smaller islands and go up the inland waterway. Your tour whetted my appetite for more.'

Adam looked at her sharply. 'It whetted my appetite, too,' he said, looking the length of her.

The tautness between them was back and Jessica said desperately, 'Adam, please! You know I meant sightseeing!'

He rammed his hands in his pockets and walked faster. 'We'll go out one day soon. We can sail over to Cumberland Island. It's a wildlife refuge that can only be reached by boat. Sidney Lanier wrote about Glynn County, you know, in his poem, "The Marshes of Glynn".' He looked out over the sea as he spoke and she had an unguarded moment to watch him. His eyes were narrowed against the glare. The wind ruffled his hair. His jawline was strong, firm, and his mouth . . . Jessica jerked her eyes away from that sensual mouth.

They went only a short distance further, before Adam stopped. 'We'd better get back. I don't like to be away from the phone too long.'

She gave him a penetrating look. 'You're worried about Dennis, aren't you?'

'I'm responsible for him, Jess, since I brought him here for this case, but I have the utmost confidence in him. He's a clever and brilliant man, and he knows what he's doing.' Steadily he looked at her, and she knew that he meant everything he said, and was reassured.

They turned to walk back towards the house. The wind, blowing from behind them now, picked up Jessica's hair and swirled it into her face, blinding her for a moment. She lost her balance and stumbled, and Adam's arm was at her waist in an instant, steadying her.

She laughed up at him, 'Do you see what happens when I leave it down?'

She was clasped against his hard body, her hands on his shoulders, and his eyes darkened as he looked into her face. She could feel the stirring muscles of his thighs in contact with her own and the strong beat of his heart.

Slowly he lowered his head. 'I see what happens to me,' he said, his voice hard.

There was no gentleness, no affection in his attitude. It was clear that this was only physical arousal. Even so Jessica's lips were raised instinctively towards his and her arms slid around his neck, when he suddenly avoided her mouth and buried his face in her hair. He held her tightly for a moment before reaching up to grab her wrists and disentangle her arms.

'Let's go back!' His long stride was taking him back the way they had come.

Jessica's eyes filled with tears and it was difficult to blink them back. She didn't know how much more of this she could stand. The constant turmoil fluctuated her senses from raging desire to rattling anger, and the ebb and flow was undermining her self-assurance. As she followed more slowly on shaky legs, her resolve strengthened to keep Adam from knowing how deeply her feelings went. It was almost impossible not to respond to him, but he mustn't know that it was more than physical for her. Back at the house she once again resumed her place at the typewriter.

Adam spoke in a brisk voice from behind her. 'I'm sorry, Jess, if I seem to have very little self-control around you. I didn't mean . . .'

'For heaven's sake, Adam,' she interrupted him glibly, 'don't make such an issue of it! The circumstances are unusual. You're an attractive man. The tension has been rather thick, but don't think you owe me anything—much less an apology. I'll try not to bother you any more!' Her voice was flippant and, except for a slight break at the end of her words, reflected none of the pain she was feeling.

'Bother me!' Adam exploded. He jerked her out of the chair and turned her into his arms. He looked down at her for a moment before his hold tightened and bruising lips covered hers punishingly.

Jessica fought him. 'No, Adam. Please, no!' Her hands were caught between their bodies and she pushed at him frantically.

'You bother me all right!' he growled against her mouth.

She turned her head to avoid his lips. 'Don't do this! I don't want it!' She was struggling, but he only held her tighter. He planted one leg between hers and pulled her towards him, making her lose her balance. She gripped the folds of his shirt to keep from falling.

The next kiss was only slightly more temperate. Her moist lips were parted in protest, and Adam took advantage of this to explore her mouth slowly and thoroughly. Then he lowered his head to the throbbing pulse in her throat.

'You don't?' he murmured. His hands burned trails across her back, slipping down to her hips to press her to the length of him.

Aflame with the sensual feelings he was arousing in her, Jessica struggled, not with him, but with herself. Part of her wanted him, but another part remembered that he had never said he loved her. She pushed against his chest with the hands still imprisoned there. The crisp hair under her fingers excited her. She tried one more time. 'No, Adam,' she insisted, but her voice was husky.

He lifted his head and dark smouldering eyes searched hers. She was aware that her expression belied her words, and she lowered her lashes to hide it from him, but it was too late.

Adam's face was like granite as he picked her up effortlessly in his arms and crossed to the sofa. He sat down holding her across his lap. When he again lowered his mouth to hers she gave up all pretence and wound her arms closely about his neck.

Jessica could hardly breathe. She was lost in a tidal wave of such intensity that it threatened to drown her.

Adam's mouth was not gentle as it travelled relentlessly over her face and throat, returning to the parted sweetness of her lips again and again. Suddenly the steel bands of his arms were no longer around her. He rested her against the arm of the sofa, leaving both his hands free to make short work of the buttons on her blouse. He smiled slightly at the front fastening of her lacy bra. Parting the two cups of lace, he stared passionately at what was revealed. 'God, you're beautiful!' His voice was rasping as his hands cupped her breasts and lifted them to his descending mouth.

She gloried in the feel of his hands caressing their fullness while his tongue traced circles around the hardening pink peaks. Then his hands moved down to span her waist, thumbs insinuating themselves in the waistband of her slacks.

He lifted his head to look at her. The flame in his eyes was burning out of control and his voice was uneven. 'Jess, I want to make love to you! Don't say no,' he groaned. 'I have a burning ache that's driving me out of my mind!' His voice rose as his fingers tightened. 'Oh, God, I want you!'

As he claimed her lips possessively once more, her hands stilled on his neck. A tear escaped from beneath her lashes and another. Pain filled her eyes. Her wish hadn't come true. He didn't love her, he only wanted her. Her heart turned to lead in her chest and the fever fanned by his touch began to die. 'No, Adam,' she said, and began to struggle again.

He was dazed for a moment and looked at her tear-streaked face uncomprehendingly. Then an uncontrollable anger convulsed his entire body. 'What do you mean, 'no', you little tease? You want me, too! Your body tells me that!' His words grated harshly. 'Look at you!'

She was reaching for the blouse to cover herself, but he grabbed both sides in his hands, holding them apart. His gaze raked her swollen breasts.

Jessica turned her head away. 'I can't handle an affair, Adam!' Her voice broke on a sob.

'How in the hell can it be an affair when we're married? And what are you crying about?' He was almost shouting.

'I'm not crying! And we're not really married. I—we—this marriage! We're going to have it annulled!'

The silence was heavy for a moment. Then Adam released her abruptly and uttered a savage epithet.

Jessica swung shaky legs to the floor and stood up, moving away from him. With trembling fingers she fumbled to fasten her bra and shirt. 'Aren't we?' she added in a small voice. She risked a look at his hard features.

'You're damned right!' His eyes pierced her. 'And the sooner the better!'

Jessica had her answer. Misery engulfed her as she turned to leave the room.

The phone rang shrilly in the silence, and Adam reached over from where he still sat on the sofa to pick up the extension. 'Yes?' he said tightly. 'Dennis! Am I glad to hear from you!'

Jessica halted on the way out of the room, swallowing her tears.

'You are? Great! No, we don't want to take any chances on exposing him.' His fingers massaged his forehead. 'Okay, I'll pick you up in the boat about four o'clock and we can be back here by dawn.' He paused to listen. 'She's here,' he stated evenly, handing the phone to Jessica, who had moved to stand beside him.

'Dennis? Are you coming home? I'm so relieved!' Tears were streaming down her cheeks.

'If you're so relieved, why are you crying, Jess? Are you all right?' The familiar voice was comforting.

'I'm fine. I can't wait to see you,' she choked, and Adam took the phone from her shaking fingers.

His mouth was grim and he sounded unusually

tired as he said, 'Dennis, she's fine. I'll see you tonight.' When he had replaced the receiver he took a deep breath and let it out slowly. He stood and shrugged his shoulders as though a great weight had been lifted from them. 'Well, Jess, it's over,' he said soberly.

Tears were still choking her and she gave a little sob. She tucked her hair behind an ear.

'Jess, I'm sorry I lost my temper. It's just that I . . .' He reached to pull her into his arms, but she evaded him and ran from the room.

Jessica closed the bedroom door behind her and leaned against it, and the dam burst. She flung herself on the bed and cried and cried, until she was totally drained.

It was over, she thought. If it would ever be over. She loved Adam with every fibre of her being. He was the breath of life to her. With the tensions of the last few days washed away by her tears, exhaustion took over and Jessica slept deeply.

A knock on the door roused her. She raised herself on one elbow and called hoarsely, 'Come in.'

Adam opened the door. Across the room his eyes took in her swollen ones and tousled hair. He sighed, and her pain was reflected in his expression. 'Jess,' he said quietly, 'we'll have to go to the dance at the club tonight as we planned. Afterwards Grace will come here to stay with you until I return with Dennis.'

'I don't want to go to a dance!' The pillow muffled her words as she buried her face in a belated attempt to hide the signs of her tears.

'This is one party I'd rather skip, too. However, we're going!' He explained patiently, 'Dennis is leaving one of our investigators on the island where they are now, to intercept further messages. He's cleared the case up from this end, but there may be shipments coming in. The smugglers won't know that there's no one to receive them. These are loose ends that must be tied up. We have to follow our plans and act as normally as possible for the protection of the operative, as well as for Dennis.'

'All right, Adam.' Jessica rolled over and sat up on the edge of the bed.

'Jess, I . . .' He took a step toward where she sat on the bed.

She flinched away from him.

Adam said harshly, 'Wear something with a high neckline! Then maybe you won't have to endure my unwelcome attentions.' He turned abruptly and left the room.

Unwelcome? If he only knew! She was longing for his attention, but only if it was given in love.

Jessica's restless night and the emotional turmoil of the last few hours had taken their toll. She would have liked nothing better than to crawl back into bed, but, sighing deeply, she went to the shower.

CHAPTER EIGHT

JESSICA dreaded this evening as she had never dreaded anything before. Still she dressed carefully, feeling for some reason that this might be the most important evening of her life. She chose a long-sleeved dress of soft lightweight ivory wool. There were tiny pearl buttons all the way down the front, from the high neckline to the hem. Just about as demure as you can get, she thought wryly. She wondered about the way it clung to the curves of her body, but shrugged. Adam had said a high neckline and it had a high neckline. She slipped her feet into gold sandals and picked up a matching handbag. Her hair was in a smooth chignon. She wore no jewellery except for the wide gold wedding band.

Jessica went into the living room to find Adam standing by the fireplace, a glass in his hand. His expression was dour as he stared into the flames.

Her breath caught in her throat at the sight of him dressed in the black tuxedo. His shoulders were so broad. She felt that they could carry any burden, no matter how heavy. For just a moment she allowed her optimistic dreams to surface. Heaven would be if they were really husband and wife, dressed to go out to dinner. She would walk across the room and wrap her arms around him. She would tell him how handsome he looked and how much she loved him. Then she would be enfolded in that strong embrace, and be warm again.

When Adam turned and saw her, he stiffened. His eyes darkened, travelling over her. He frowned at the long row of tiny buttons. 'Very virginal! You don't look much like a woman on her honeymoon. You're too unruffled.'

His sarcastic tone shattered her mood of a moment ago. 'Stop sniping! You didn't have to marry me!' she said, angrily fighting tears.

Adam took a deep breath. 'Let's go!' he answered sharply, setting his glass down with a thump on the low table.

They entered the club in a jam of people to the sound of music. A young man, who had obviously visited the bar too often this early in the evening, jostled Jessica. Adam's hand went immediately to her waist to steady her, then was quickly withdrawn as though it had been burned.

'Watch where you're going!' Adam muttered furiously.

'Sorry, Mr Oakman.' The youngsters gave an offhand apology while looking curiously at Jessica.

The maître d' had consulted his seating chart and was leading them to their table when Jessica heard a low, husky voice behind them.

'Adam, darling!'

He turned. 'Hello, Vanessa.'

Jessica froze, then looked over her shoulder. It was the woman from the picture—only more so! She was one of the most striking girls Jessica had ever seen. She wound her arms around Adam's neck and kissed him thoroughly. His hand went to her back with obvious familiarity.

This was Vanessa! Jessica's face whitened as she watched them. Her fists clenched until her nails dug into her palms painfully. A picture of a fiancée was one thing, but all of a sudden she was devastated at the prospect of meeting the flesh-and-blood woman.

Adam steadily observed her white face as he disengaged Vanessa's arms. His hand still at her back, he led her to where Jessica was standing.

'Jessica, this is Vanessa Lord; Vanessa, my wife, Jessica.'

She was taller than Jessica. Her hair was a shade between black and brown that exactly matched her eyes. She wore a clinging red dress, deceptively simple, which must have cost a fortune. It was slit on one side showing quite a lot of well-shaped leg and was daringly low, but that neckline didn't seem to bother Adam. He was smiling warmly at her.

She finally tore her adoring gaze from Adam and acknowledged the introduction. Her eyes were flint as they raked Jessica and dismissed her. A deep throaty laugh accompanied her words. 'Oh yes, darling, I've heard about the quick little ceremony.'

She managed to make it sound very cheap, and Jessica longed to slap that derisive smirk off her face. Instead she lifted her chin a bit higher. Surprisingly, when her eyes met Adam's, he was smiling slightly, watching her with something approaching approval.

'I just can't believe it!' Vanessa continued, oblivious to their exchange. 'I go to New York to shop for a week and come home to find you married!' A beautiful pout formed her lips. 'What was the hurry?'

Jessica didn't wait to hear his answer. She mumbled something and hurried after the maître d' to the table that had been reserved for them.

As she sat down in the chair the harassed man held for her, she saw Kevin Short wave from across the room and rise to come towards her. Gratefully she gave a little wave back. She felt as if he was a lifeline.

'Jessica, it's good to see you!' He put his hand on her shoulder and leaned down as though to kiss her. Jessica shrank from the contact.

'Get your hands off my wife, Short!' Adam spoke behind them through clenched teeth.

Kevin was almost as startled as Jessica was at the anger in his voice. 'Sorry, Adam. I was only greeting an old friend.' He straightened. 'Jessica, save a dance for me, will you?' he said, smiling down at her boldly.

Jessica found her voice. 'Thank you, Kevin, I'd love to.' After the way Adam had devoured

Vanessa with his eyes, he needn't think he was going to play the indignant husband with her! Kevin moved away.

'I don't want you to dance with him,' Adam said, taking his chair opposite her. He was curt and aloof, so she matched his attitude.

'Well, that's too bad, because I've already accepted!' she snapped. 'Besides, I'm sure Vanessa will be delighted to entertain you!'

Adam's eyes gleamed. 'I'm sure she will. Vanessa's always entertaining,' he said smoothly.

The waiter appeared to take their order, but before Adam could reply Vanessa came over.

'Darling, two of our party haven't shown up. Why don't you and your . . . bride join our table?' The hesitation in her request made a clear point of her scepticism. Adam had stood at her approach, and blood-red nails rested on his arm while she looked at him appealingly.

'I don't think so, Vanessa. Thanks anyway. Jessica and I are having a small celebration.' He smiled warmly at the dark-haired girl. The regret in his voice was sincere.

'A celebration? Wonderful!' She didn't sound as though she thought it was wonderful at all, mused Jessica.

Vanessa purred, 'I'm sure your bride wouldn't want to deprive your old friends of the pleasure of helping you celebrate.'

With a raised eyebrow, Adam looked at Jessica. 'Do you want to move to their table?' A celebration, he had said. A celebration of the end of their marriage? Had he already told Vanessa the circumstances? She didn't think she could stand to sit here alone with him, trying to make casual conversation, when she loved him so much.

'That would be fun, Adam. I'm in the mood for a crowd anyway.' She had to force the words through a dry throat, but she continued with spirit, 'Are you with Kevin?'

'Yes,' Vanessa answered, then turned again to Adam. 'Disillusioned bride already, darling? You must be slipping!' she laughed. 'You never had any trouble with me!'

Adam answered, never taking his eyes from Jessica, 'It does look that way, doesn't it?'

A blaze of dislike welled up in Jessica. This girl was like a creepy snake, wriggling and writhing against him, an insinuating Jezebel! Couldn't Adam see through all that affectation? Jessica was disgusted. How could he be attracted to someone like her? Then she answered her own question. Look at her. She's gorgeous! And that dress! Invitation in every line and slit! Why, it made the little black dress she had worn in Washington look puritanical.

Adam's jaw had hardened. 'By all means, Jess, let's join the others if you'd like to.'

His fingers were tight on her arm as they followed Vanessa to a large round table in one corner of the ballroom.

Vanessa indicated a place to her right. 'Sit here by me, darling. Kevin can sit on the other side of your bride.'

How did she manage to make that word a sneer every time she said it? thought Jessica.

Vanessa's hand rested on Adam's arm. 'He may have better luck entertaining her. I know he'll enjoy trying. He was quite smitten, I believe, before you snatched her away from him.' She leaned towards him, smiling.

The remark was completely off base. She and Kevin had been merely friends, but maybe it explained his 'we' on the phone this morning. He probably couldn't wait to tell Vanessa about the marriage. Kevin was a bit of a gossip.

'Vanessa has her claws out tonight, Jessica. Let's dance,' Kevin whispered in her ear, and Adam gave her a burning glare as she rose.

She danced with Kevin and one or two others in their party, being determinedly cheerful, while Adam's expression became blacker as the evening wore on.

The food might as well have been cardboard for all the taste it had for Jessica. She could only force down a few bites. The muscles in her cheeks were stiff from smiling when she didn't feel at all like smiling. A nagging pain at the base of her skull indicated the onset of a headache. While they were waiting for dessert, Kevin asked her to dance and Adam stood abruptly and said, 'Vanessa, shall we?'

As they moved to the music, Jessica's eyes were continuously drawn to the other couple. He hadn't asked her to dance a single time! Her head was really beginning to throb now and she felt sick. She stumbled slightly and Kevin caught her close.

He murmured into her ear, 'What's wrong?' Over his shoulder she glimpsed a threatening look in Adam's expression. She really was ill.

'It's the heat and smoke in here, I guess. I have a splitting headache.' She raised a shaking hand to her temple.

Kevin danced her across the floor to the french doors leading outside. As he reached in front of her to open one Adam, with Vanessa in tow, appeared beside them.

'Where do you think you're going?' His hand was gripping her elbow, and she had to fight to keep from leaning weakly against him, from turning her face into that broad chest and clinging to him.

'Darling, you shouldn't ask such silly questions,' Vanessa simpered.

Jessica stiffened and pulled her arm away from Adam's grip.

Kevin answered for her, 'Jessica has a headache. We were going out for a breath of fresh air.'

'We'll all go,' Adam said tersely.

The night was mild for January. As they sauntered along the terrace, they could see the lights from the causeway twinkling in the distance.

Jessica took great gulps of the cool air and savoured the fragrance of new-mown grass. She stopped walking and leaned on her elbows on the stone balustrade, looking up to the stars. Her head still throbbed, but the faint nausea was passing.

The men moved away and Vanessa began to question Jessica about the marriage. 'Where did you and Adam meet?' she asked, in that honey-dripping voice. Her hands smoothed the red dress where it clung to her hips.

Jessica gave the same evasive answer she had given earlier to Kevin. 'Adam and my brother have been friends since they were in college.'

'Isn't it strange that he's never mentioned you to me?'

Jessica's head was really pounding now and she felt she would scream if she didn't get away from this girl. Then she smiled at herself. She couldn't lose control here—Vanessa would love that!

Vanessa saw the smile and didn't like it. 'I asked you a question!' she spat venomously.

Jessica answered calmly, 'I don't think it's so strange. He's never mentioned you to me either.' Not by name, she amended mentally.

Vanessa stared at her rudely. 'There's something curious about this hasty wedding, and I intend to find out what! Adam and I have been very close and he's never gone in for ingénues before. I happen to know that he prefers experience!' she declared with assurance.

Jessica knew she was behaving like a cat, but she couldn't stop herself as she said sweetly, 'Most men do, I believe, to play around with, but perhaps when it came to marriage he wanted something different.' She let her eyes roam over the red dress. 'Quite different.'

The other girl was speechless, but when she glanced behind Jessica she let big tears well in her eyes. 'Oh, Adam! I'm afraid your little bride doesn't like me.'

The two men had come up behind her. Had they heard her remarks? Jessica had her answer when Adam scowled angrily.

Kevin interjected before Adam could speak. 'Are you feeling better? Do you want to go in?'

She nodded numbly.

'Let's change partners,' said Adam as they re-entered the ballroom.

Jessica found herself in his arms. His breath against her temple was doing devastating things to her senses. Forcing herself to concentrate on other people around them, she met the triumphant leer in Vanessa's eyes.

'I'm sorry I spoke to Vanessa like that,' she mumbled.

Adam didn't reply. He was holding her stiffly.

'I'd like to sit down, Adam,' she said, her voice quavering.

'What's the matter? Can't you stand my arms

around you for the few minutes it takes to dance? Or maybe it's because I don't hold you as close as Short does.'

She realised that he was furious, probably because of her aversion to Vanessa.

He jerked her so close she could hardly breathe. 'What have you told him about this marriage? He doesn't seem to be taking it very seriously, and you looked as though you enjoyed his hands all over you!'

Suddenly she was gloriously, blazingly angry! She leaned back as far as his arms would allow and glowered at him. 'Well, you finally condescend to speak to me—I'm honoured! Those are practically the only words I've heard from you since we sat down to dinner!'

Adam's arms slackened and he gaped at her in astonishment as she continued, her voice shaking with blazing fury.

'And furthermore, Kevin's hands were not all over me, but yours surely were all over that . . . Vanessa! She tells me she knows you very well.'

Adam's face hardened at her low-voiced tirade. 'Be quiet, Jess!' he muttered. 'You don't know what you're talking about.'

But Jessica was determined to finish. 'She must be the fiancée you referred to. Well, you're welcome to each other! You obviously didn't object to *her* neckline!'

'Shut up!' Adam grated through clenched teeth. 'Let's get out of here!' He was barely holding on to his own temper. 'I've got to leave soon, and Grace will be waiting for you.'

'I don't need a babysitter and I'm not leaving! Take Vanessa! Then the two of you can say a romantic goodbye. She's certainly dressed for romance, or whatever!'

He took her wrist in a bruising grip, and heads turned as he half-dragged her to the door.

'Adam, don't!' she hissed. She was beginning to regret her outburst already.

'Jessica, I'm warning you.' He had stopped and was glaring down at her. 'If you say one more word, I'm going to wallop the daylights out of you right here!' he said, his voice dangerously low. The compelling, primitive blaze flamed from his eyes.

'My bag,' she said in a very small voice.

He took a deep breath before he replied, 'I'll get it. Stay here!'

Jessica stood where she was, enduring the curious stares of the people around her with a proud little tilt to her chin, but she was fighting to hold back tears.

Adam returned in only a moment with the small gold bag in his hand. He guided her with a hand in the small of her back, from the ballroom to the foyer.

'Does it make you feel better to act like a caveman?' she said sarcastically when they were through the doors and out into the cool darkness.

Without answering Adam pulled her along to

the car and shoved her in, slamming the door furiously. He was tearing at his tie as he went around in front of the car to his side and he rammed it into the pocket of his dinner jacket before he got in.

Gravel spun from beneath the wheels when he accelerated out of the parking lot. He drove at a reckless pace along the highway, unbuttoning the top button of his shirt with one hand. His fingers wrapped around the steering wheel in a strangling grip, the knuckles white. He was breathing like a long-distance runner. A black scowl furrowed his brow, his eyes were narrowed.

Jessica wiped away a tear and stared down at her clenched hands in her lap. She fingered the heavy gold wedding ring absently, turning it round and round.

As they pulled into the driveway he slammed on the brakes, almost throwing her out of her seat. She put a hand on the dashboard to catch herself.

'What's the matter? Is it too heavy for you?' he scowled.

Her eyes flew to meet his in the dimness of the car. 'What?' she asked, not understanding.

'It's easy to see,' he continued, sarcasm dripping from his tones, 'you don't like the restriction of that ring, do you?'

Jessica knew she shouldn't answer, it would be wiser to ignore his gibe, but her anger matched his. 'Well, what about you? You don't even wear a ring,' she taunted.

'That's your fault! Why didn't you give me one?'

She caught her breath. The silence stretched. Her mouth went dry as she looked at him unbelieving. 'Adam . . .' she croaked. A small bud of hope flowered, only to be crushed at his next words.

'Forget I said that!' he shot out with finality.

Jessica felt numb. Her fumbling fingers tried to grip the handle of the door.

'I won't come back with Dennis,' he said, barely controlling his temper. 'You may as well pack. He can pick you up and take you home, then tomorrow you can start your annulment proceedings.' He stared out through the windshield as he spoke, never once looking at her white face.

'Yes—off with the old, on with the new. You'll be free then to marry Vanessa. I'm sure she's much more appealing to you than I am!' Her voice was rising hysterically, but she couldn't swallow the challenge.

Adam was out of the car in an instant. Jessica opened the door, but he was around it before she could get out. He jerked her up and pinned her to the side of the car with his hips, one hand on each side of her.

'My God—appealing! I'll show you what's appealing!' What little control he had been able to hold on to suddenly snapped. His hands were in her hair, ripping the pins out.

'Ouch! Adam, you're hurting!' She tried to push his hands away.

'I'd like to hurt you!' he bellowed. His fingers were combing through her long hair. 'I'd like you to feel some of the pain I've been feeling ever since I met you!'

Then his hands moved to the neckline of the dress. 'All night you've deliberately driven me insane, by flirting with Kevin Short. You of all people know how important tonight is, but I couldn't concentrate on any of the things I should have my mind on! All I could think about was how long it would take me to undo all these damned buttons!'

Dumbfounded, Jessica stared at him. What was he saying? She gasped. 'Adam, I didn't mean . . .'

'Don't tell me you didn't mean them to be a challenge! You must have know they'd be more of an invitation than the most revealing neckline!'

His hands were shaking as he concentrated on the buttons. Then he lifted his head. The smouldering light in his eyes held her prisoner as his voice lowered to become a hypnotic murmur. 'The thought of your breasts in my hands and my lips on that damned mole has just about driven me crazy. I wanted to feel your lips open under mine, your arms around my neck, and the length of your body against me. I wanted to undress you slowly and take you to bed and lock out the rest of the world. That's what's appealing!' His hands on her shoulders gave her a shake before his mouth came down on hers and he crushed her to him. He caressed her back from shoulder to thigh, kindling flames at every point he touched.

He hadn't got very far with the buttons, and it was a good thing, because at that moment light spilled from the open doorway.

'Adam? Jessica? Is that you?' Grace's voice was like a knife between them.

Jessica could hardly stand as he thrust her away.

'Get inside, and don't be here when I come back if you don't want to take the consequences!' he blazed hoarsely. He went around and opened the door on the driver's side. The car was between them now, and they faced each other across the hood.

Jessica sought for a glimmer of warmth in those rugged features. She thought she saw one. For a fleeting second there was a flash of pain in Adam's eyes before the shuttered look returned. Her voice trembling she said, 'Adam, we . . . I . . . your fiancée . . .'

His eyes pierced her. 'Dammit, Jessica there never was a fiancée! You should have known that!' He got into the car and slammed the door, then reversing quickly, he roared out of the driveway.

Jessica stood there staring after the disappearing tail-lights. Her thoughts were whirling, but her body felt as though it had been turned to stone.

Finally she turned towards the house, where Grace stood on the porch watching her. Jessica gripped the railing as she slowly mounted the steps.

'Jessica, are you all right?' asked Grace.

'Yes, thank you, I'm fine, Grace,' she answered in a monotone. 'At least, I think I am.'

CHAPTER NINE

HOURS later Jessica still lay on her back staring at the ceiling. The white dress had been discarded for a comfortable pair of jeans and a sweater. It was almost dawn. The night had been a long one and the day promised to be even longer.

Dennis walked into the room. His clothes were wrinkled and a day's growth of beard darkened his rugged face. There were dark circles under his eyes, but he grinned at Jessica, saying, 'Well, Mrs Oakman?'

'Oh, Dennis!' She jumped up and threw herself into his arms. 'Dennis, I've been so worried. Thank God you're all right!' she cried.

He held her and asked gently, looking down at her bent head, 'Are *you* all right, Jess?'

'I'm fine,' she replied, smiling up at him.

Violet eyes met weary blue ones. 'Now that you're back, I'm fine.' But her lip trembled.

'Adam explained everything to me, Sis,' Dennis said heavily. 'Please try not to worry. It's all over now and we'll soon take care of getting you an annulment.' He sounded so tired, so very tired.

Jessica was silent for a moment, then, pulling out of his arms, she asked carefully, 'Is that what Adam said he wanted?' Her hands were clenched together over her stomach. They betrayed her nervousness, but she had come to a decision during the long hours of the night.

Dennis motioned for her to sit down. She perched on the edge of the bed while he took a chair. 'Jess, Adam is a very close friend. He's like a brother to me, and you're my sister, so I don't want to see either one of you hurt. Let's go home.' He leaned forward, resting his elbows on his knees, to study her earnestly.

She looked at the face of her dear big brother and said softly, 'This is one predicament you can't help me out of. I love Adam, Dennis. For a while I didn't think he cared, but tonight . . . no, last night, just before he left . . .' She paused and a determined gleam lit her eyes. 'I'm not going with you. I have to stay and see him one more time, at least. After all,' she teased weakly, 'this is what you wanted, isn't it? Weren't you playing matchmaker?'

Dennis laughed without humour. He raked a

hand through his light brown hair and relaxed against the back cushion of the chair. 'Yes. I thought the two of you would be great together. Adam used to come to the house in Washington a lot when you were away at school,' Dennis said thoughtfully. 'He seemed to be fascinated by that portrait of you. Of course, at that time you were so young that I didn't think about introducing you, but just before I came down here to take this job Adam mentioned that he'd like to meet you.'

'He did?' Jessica glowed. 'Oh, thank you for telling me!'

'But, Jess, you've only known each other a few days,' he argued. 'I didn't plan it like this.'

'But this is the way it happened, Dennis. I wouldn't have planned it like this either, but it's happened, and for me it's for ever. So you see, I have to find out . . . I have to stay and see Adam.'

The sincerity in her voice and eyes had almost convinced him, but he tried one more time. 'He's with the Federal Marshals, Jess. Warrants have to be prepared, and it could take most of the day. Why don't you come home with me and we'll see Adam together, later?'

'Dennis, I am home,' she said gently.

Dennis stood and crossed to pull her up into his arms again. His voice was loving when he said, 'I guess you are at that.' He put out a hand to push back her tousled hair and gave her a wry smile. 'Adam told me about the folks' trip. How we're ever going to explain this to them, I don't know, but I hope it works out for you and Adam, Jess.' His arm tightened, and he hesitated before continuing, 'Adam keeps his own counsel, so he hasn't said anything to me. For what it's worth, though, I've never seen him so distracted. He's always had a certain success with women, but none of them has ever had this effect on him—at least, not since I've known him. I think he was insisting on the annulment so that you wouldn't feel tied to him by circumstances.'

'I'm tied to him by love, not circumstances, and I have to tell him so, Dennis.'

'Yes, I guess you do.' He raked his hand through his hair again. 'God, I'm tired!'

'Dennis—I'm sorry! I didn't ask ... Did everything go well? Did you catch the smugglers?'

His tired features relaxed. 'Everything went perfectly! It was a big operation, bigger even than we'd suspected. In fact we'll be rounding up the participants for a long time. Everyone we've arrested so far is leading us to another connection. With my testimony and that of my truck-driver friend we'll put them all behind bars for a long time.'

'That's wonderful! I'm very proud of my big brother!' She hugged him. 'Now why don't you go home and get some sleep before you fall out on your feet?'

'I wish I could! I have to go back to the Marshal's office, too, after I have a shower and change clothes.'

Jessica walked with him to the front door.

'Grace has already left. Will you be okay here by yourself?' Dennis asked.

'I'll be fine.' She smiled with confidence.

'Do you want me to tell Adam you're waiting for him?'

Jessica thought for a minute. 'No, I don't think so. He has enough on his mind.' She twinkled up at him. 'Besides, I'd like to surprise him!'

He laughed. 'You'll probably do that.'

Suddenly she had a thought. 'Dennis, could you bring me something from the house on your way back to town?' She explained what she wanted.

He smiled tenderly down at her. 'You really do mean this, don't you?'

She said soberly, 'Yes, Dennis, I do.'

When he had gone Jessica took the blue windbreaker from the hall tree and let herself out of the sliding glass doors. The sea breeze was benevolent on her face as she wandered to the water's edge. The sun, just setting out on today's journey across the sky, coloured the ocean a molten gold, and her heart lifted with the great red ball. It was going to be a beautiful day!

Dennis was back in less than an hour. Jessica met him at the door to take the small box he brought her, and opened it briefly before putting it into the pocket of the windbreaker.

'Thanks, Dennis. You look better!'

He had showered and shaved. Laughing

wearily, he said, 'I'll feel better after about twenty-four hours' sleep! But I won't get it until we finish with the Marshal, so I'd better go. Call me, Jess.'

'I will, Dennis. I love you.'

He kissed her cheek and smiled. 'I love you too, sis. Good luck!'

After Dennis had left again, the house felt doubly empty. Jessica roamed from room to room absorbing the presence of the man who lived here.

Suddenly she thought of something she could do. Rummaging in the kitchen drawers, she found a hammer and nail and returned with them to the bedroom. She dragged her suitcase from the back of the closet, and took out the painting. A lump formed in her throat as she looked at it through blurred eyes. On the wall facing the door she hammered home the nail.

When the painting was hung, she stood back, hands on her hips, to admire it again. Peter Vance was going to be famous one day.

The morning dragged on. Jessica searched for tasks to keep herself busy.

After lunch she showered and dressed carefully in a beautiful flowing caftan of striped jewel colours. It was slit on both sides to the knee, and the mandarin collar closed with tiny Oriental frogs. She had washed and dried her hair, leaving it free to tumble over her shoulders.

This waiting was nerve-racking. Jessica sat on

the sofa and picked up a magazine. She read it all the way through without knowing a thing she had read, and finally threw it down in dusgust. For a while she busied herself in the kitchen with preparations for dinner, but she could only stretch out a chore for so long. Eventually she found herself back in the living room. Moving to the stereo in the corner, she selected a record to put on. The beautiful classical music filled the room and she reached to turn the volume to a background level, smiling to herself. Adam liked to hear his music. She wandered over to look out at the ocean. It was almost dark. What time would he be home?

The shrill ringing of the telephone startled her, and she jumped to answer it, hoping it was Adam. 'Mrs Oakman?'

Jessica swallowed her disappointment at the sound of a strange woman's voice. 'Yes, this is she.'

'Mrs Oakman, this is Mrs Eaton. I'm a nurse at the Glynn County Hospital. Your husband has been involved in an accident. I'm sorry to have to break it to you like this, but can you come right away?'

The blood drained from Jessica's face and an unbearable pain shot through her. She doubled over and her knees gave way as she sank into a chair. 'What . . . How . . .' Her hand went to her forehead. 'Wait—I'll come! Of course I'll come.' The room tilted and she struggled to clear her mind. 'Oh, I don't have a car!' she cried. 'I'll have to call a taxi.'

'Just a minute, Mrs Oakman.' Jessica could hear muffled voices at the other end of the line before the woman came back on. 'One of our interns is just going off duty. If you like, he'll come for you. He can be there in about five minutes.'

'Oh, please! Thank you, thank you so much—Mrs Eaton, is it? I'll be ready.' Jessica slammed down the phone and raced for the bedroom, pulling at the buttons of the caftan as she went. Tears streamed down her face. She opened the closet and grabbed for something to wear. Two nightgowns and a pair of jeans were thrown to the floor before she finally found a skirt and sweater.

'Adam, Adam,' she moaned. 'Five minutes! I've got to hurry!' The skirt was zipped, the sweater over her head, and she was reaching for her shoes when she froze.

Five minutes. The hospital was over the causeway in Brunswick, at least twenty minutes away. How could the intern be here in five minutes? What was going on?

Jessica reached up with both hands to dash the tears away. The anguish she felt at the idea of Adam's being hurt was getting in the way of her reasoning. She sat on the edge of the bed, trying to piece it all together.

Mrs Eaton had said she was calling from the

hospital. Suddenly her blood ran cold and she took a deep breath. Clutching her shoes, she hurried back into the living room. She remembered something Dennis had once told her and calmly picked up the telephone directory. She dialled the number of the hospital and cradled the receiver between her shoulder and ear, while she slipped her shoes on to her feet.

The receptionist was very pleasant. No, there was not a Mrs Eaton employed there. No, not even in the emergency room, and there had been no accident patients brought in this afternoon.

Jessica put down the phone with a cold hand and sat staring at it. So that was it—they wanted her! Dennis still had to testify! She had better get out of here. But first . . .

Again she thumbed through the directory. Marshal, Federal? No, no! Government? United States! Yes, here it was. Quickly she dialled.

'Federal Marshal's office,' a woman answered.

'May I speak to Adam Oakman or . . . or Dennis Gentry, please? And please, hurry. It's an emergency . . . I think!'

'Jessica? Is that you? This is Grace. What's wrong?' There was a commotion on the line.

'Oh, Grace, I'm not sure, but I think . . . I had a phone call. From the hospital—they said Adam was hurt. But I called back and there was no Mrs Eaton.' Jessica rushed to get the words out. She hoped Grace would understand the disjointed phrases. 'And she said an intern would pick me up in five minutes. Grace, I'm scared.'

'It's not Grace, it's me, honey, and I heard you. Now listen, Jess . . .'

'Adam! Oh, Adam! You're not hurt?' She was weeping now and could only whisper, 'You're all right.'

'Jessica—listen to me!' His voice was strained, harsh. 'I have a man watching your parents' house. I'll get him on the radio. Just lock yourself in, darling. He'll take care of the rest, but don't open the door for anyone.'

'But . . . but, Adam . . .' Tears of relief interfered with her voice, 'I'm not there. I'm at home!'

There was a deathly silence. 'God!' he breathed.

'Adam?' She wiped her face with a palm.

'Jessica,' he said hoarsely. 'Jessica . . .' Then she could hear the strength returning to his voice when he ordered, 'Listen carefully, Jess. You've got to get out of the house, right now. Hide! Go out the back, to the beach.' He took a breath and said clearly, deliberately, 'Along to your right about a hundred yards is a stand of palmettos. Get in there and stay down! Do you hear me?'

'Yes,' she sniffed.

'Stay in the sawgrass as much as you can so you won't leave footprints. Jessica, do you understand?' he said sharply.

'Yes, Adam, I understand.'

'You can do it, darling. I'm on my way!' He slammed down the phone, not waiting for a response.

As Jessica replaced the receiver with a trembling hand she saw car lights reflected in the narrow window above the front door. She caught her breath and quickly fled through the glass doors, stopping only to close them, and slip out of her shoes again. Quietly she crossed the wooden deck and ran down the steps.

The sound of the doorbell reached her ears faintly as she raced across the dunes and down the beach towards the palmettos.

'You can do it, darling.' His words set up a chant in her brain. 'Darling, darling!'

When she came to the spot Adam had described she was gasping for breath but didn't pause in her flight. On her hands and knees she crawled in under the thick spiky leaves. She kept her face down, but thorn-like tips tore at her hair and sweater. She kept going until she was well back into them. Then she sank back on her knees. Thank goodness, it was dark. She struggled to quiet her breathing. The scrub palmetto had closed in behind her. If she stayed very still . . .

A moment later she saw the flicker of a flashlight beam through the undergrowth and heard a muffled curse. She held her breath, trembling. Had she stayed in the grasses? She couldn't remember. And somewhere she had dropped her shoes. She sat frozen in fear.

The lights finally turned back towards the house and Jessica sighed with overwhelming relief, but didn't move.

The cold began to creep into her bones under the lightweight sweater. She didn't know how long she huddled there, but all at once there were lights and voices, lots of voices. Adam's she thought, but couldn't be sure; and another voice, she couldn't believe, calling her name.

She was scrabbling, crawling, trying to get out of her nest. 'Daddy, Daddy!' she cried. 'Here I am!'

Then she was free of the palmetto, tumbling down in the sand, and strong arms picked her up and held her. The harshness of the searchlights hurt her eyes and she buried her face against him.

'Jess, Jessica, baby! Are you all right?' Her father lifted her face to the light, smoothed back her tangled hair. Dennis was there, too, on her other side.

'Oh, Daddy, it was so awful!' She buried her face again in his chest.

The loving arms tightened around her shoulders. 'I know, baby, I know, but it's all over now. They caught the devils who were after you and they won't bother anyone for a long time,' he growled.

'Caught them? Who?' Jessica lifted her head. 'Daddy, why are you here?' She had suddenly remembered that the arms which held her were supposed to be on the other side of the world. 'Is Mother with you?' She was confused.

'Calm down, Jess,' Dennis put in. 'We'll explain it all later. Let's get you back to the house.'

As she turned she came face to face with Adam. His lips tightened and there was a bruise on his cheek. His pallor was alarming. Deep lines of fatigue scored his face and his eyes were sunken. He looked at her with a burning gaze.

Jessica pulled herself out of her father's arms to go to him on shaky legs, but he stiffened and seemed to withdraw as she approached.

'Adam,' she whispered, 'are you all right?' She lifted her hand to the bruise.

Though she touched it lightly he winced and grabbed her wrist, forcing her hand away from his face. His expression was taut. He handed her the shoes she had dropped. 'I'm fine, Jess, and so are you, now that your parents are home.'

She flinched at the expressionless tone. 'But, Adam, I thought ... you said ...' The tears noticeable in her voice threatened to spill from her eyes.

His voice was harsh as he dropped her wrist. 'It's over, Jess. Go home.' He turned away. His orders to the rest of the men were clipped. 'Let's get these lights packed up!'

Jessica, urged on by Dennis on one side and her father on the other, made her way back up the beach. She turned once to look back.

Adam's shoulders were slumped, his hands in his pockets as he listened to a man who was talking urgently to him. He didn't come into the house with them.

On wooden legs Jessica went down the hallway to his mother's bedroom. Numbly she pulled out her suitcases and started to pack, folding each item carefully, placing it in the suitcase as if her life depended on neatness. The tears of reaction had begun to fall. As she packed she wiped her cheeks with the backs of her hands.

What could she do? She had thought Adam cared. The million years ago that he had brought her home from the dance, she had been so sure, but on the beach his cold indifference swept away her confidence.

Dennis came into the room. 'Can I help you?' he asked quietly.

She shook her head and looked around the room helplessly before meeting his eyes. 'Oh, Dennis, what can I do? I don't want to leave. He looks terrible. How did he get that bruise?'

'We arrived just as two men were getting into their car. I thought Adam would half kill them before the marshals pulled him off, but one of the men landed a blow.'

Jessica winced and her hand went to her cheek as though she were the one who had been hit.

'It's nothing serious, Jess, but we're all exhausted. Let's go home. You can talk to Adam tomorrow.' Dennis picked up her suitcases and she followed him out of the room.

At the door she paused, looking back. The

painting on the wall caught her eye and she stared at it for a minute. Should she take it with her? Could she bear to leave it? Her eyes blurred. Then she shrugged and followed Dennis down the hall.

She entered her parents' house with her tight-lipped father. He was obviously very upset over something, but she had no curiousity right now to find out why.

Her mother met them at the door. She took one look at Jessica's white face and quietly led the way upstairs.

While Jessica stripped off her ruined sweater and skirt, her mother ran a tub of hot water. She still hadn't asked any questions, and Jessica was grateful. 'Thanks, Mother.' Her voice broke on a sob. 'I'm very glad you're home,' she said as she sank down in the water.

'I'm very glad, too, dear. Just relax for a few minutes. I'll be right back.'

'Ummm.' Jessica closed her eyes and immersed herself in the warmth, banishing all thought from her mind.

She roused a short while later when she heard the faint wail of a siren. Jerkily she sat up, and looked around her, disorientated. What was she doing here? She should be with Adam. Then she remembered. Sighing deeply, she stood up and reached for a giant fluffy towel.

When her mother returned with a tray, Jessica was brushing her hair with slow rhythmic strokes. She had pulled on a jump suit of soft pink velour.

Her mother deposited the tray on a table by the bed. 'I've brought hot chocolate. Coffee might keep you awake.'

'Mother, I . . .' her voice was a whisper, 'I know you want an explanation.' She put down the brush.

'Jess dear,' her mother met her eyes in the mirror, 'it can wait. We can sort it all out tomorrow. I know you've been through a terrible ordeal and what you need now is rest. We love you, and we're here.'

Jessica turned and put her arms around her mother. 'Thank you,' she choked. 'I still don't understand why you're home, but I'm so glad you are.'

'When we talked to you last week you didn't sound quite like yourself. We should have come straight home then, but when we did decide to, we caught the first plane out.' Her mother gave her a hug and turned to leave. 'Now, young lady, drink your hot chocolate and go to bed. We'll talk tomorrow,' she said with mock severity.

Jessica gave her a weak smile. 'You have to be the most wonderful mother in the world!'

Tears welled in her mother's eyes. 'And you have to be the most wonderful daughter,' she said as she left the room, closing the door softly behind her.

An hour later Jessica was still dressed and

awake in the darkened room. She had curled up in the window seat looking out over the ocean. The tears which might have provided some relief would not come. Her mother had been right about the ordeal, but mistaken as to its cause. A deep burning ache in her chest made it hard to breathe. In this house, full of a loving family, Jessica felt empty and abandoned without Adam.

She rested her forehead against the cool windowpane, staring into the night with dry eyes.

Light spilled on to the terrace from a window in the study below. Dennis and their parents must still be talking, but no sound reached her ears, until she heard the sharp closing of a door.

She clasped her arms around her knees and buried her face in them. Adam, Adam . . . why did you send me away?

There were footsteps on the stairs. They approached her room and the door opened softly behind her. 'I'm going to bed in a minute, Daddy,' she said without lifting her head.

A hoarse but amused voice answered her. 'Yes, you are, but not here.'

Jessica's head jerked around. 'Adam!' she whispered, not able to believe her eyes.

His bulk was silhouetted in the light from the doorway. She didn't move, but her wide eyes drank in the sight of him coming slowly towards her. A tiny spark of hope flared as his words finally registered, and she held her breath.

He stopped a few feet away and stood looking down at her, his hands rammed into the pockets of his jeans. She couldn't see his expression, but she felt him take a deep shuddering breath before he asked huskily, 'Will you come home with me, Jess?'

'Yes,' Jessica answered without hesitation, 'of course I will. But . . . but why . . .'

Her question was lost as he took the last few steps and pulled her up and into his arms. His lips crushed hers hungrily.

Jessica was weak with relief. Her arms wound around his waist, clinging to him. They held on to each other as though they were drowning. Adam's hard hands moulded her to him desperately.

He finally dragged his mouth away from hers to bury his face in her neck. A large hand tangled in her hair and held her head to his chest. 'I love you, Jess. I love you, my darling. From the first moment I saw you and until the end of our lives, I love you,' he murmured hoarsely.

Jessica swallowed tears of happiness to answer, her voice breaking. 'And I love you, Adam, in the same way, in the same instant.' She pulled away to look up into his face, and his arms tightened again urgently as though even that minute distance was unbearable to him.

'Let's go home,' he groaned against her cheek.

'Yes, yes, let's go home.' Joy lifted her voice.

'Do you have to pack?' he asked, loosening his

arms to look around the room, and his eyes lit on the suitcases.

'I never unpacked,' she answered, smiling up at him.

Adam groaned again and gave her a quick hard kiss. Then he pushed her ahead of him out of the room and picked up the cases.

'I should tell somebody that I'm leaving,' she said, hesitating when they reached the front door.

'They know,' Adam told her firmly. 'I told them I had come for you.'

'Adam, why did you send me away?' Jessica asked in a small voice.

He heaved a great sigh and nudged her along with the suitcase. 'Come on. I'll tell you in the car.'

Jessica opened the door of the sports car and climbed in while Adam stowed her luggage in the trunk. When he got in beside her, he put the keys into the ignition but didn't start the car. Instead he turned to look at her, laying his arm across the back of her seat. His hand stroked her hair. 'Jess, telling you to leave was the hardest thing I've ever done in my life. I felt as though I were cutting off my right arm. It hurt! Hurt—God, it was agony! I'd been wild at the thought of you in danger, and when we found you unharmed all I wanted to do was to take you in my arms and hold you for ever.'

Jessica winced at the pain in his face but her pain had been real, too. She lowered her head.

'Then why did you? You must have known I wanted to stay with you.'

The hand that had rested on the steering wheel came forward to cradle her face, lifting it so that he could look into her eyes. 'My darling, when you called the Marshal's office your father was there. He and your mother came in this afternoon and I had that man watching their house. He told your father where Dennis and I were.' His fingers laced through her hair, and he smiled wryly as he continued. 'I've always gotten along well with your parents, but when your father found out that you and I were married he exploded!' Adam sighed and reached over to start the car. 'He wouldn't give me a chance to explain.'

When they had reached the highway he spoke again. 'I'm not surprised your father was such a successful lawyer. He ranted at me until he even had me convinced I was an underhanded scoundrel, taking advantage of an innocent young beauty. And then you called. God, I've never been so scared in my life! And he was too, Jess. I guess I can understand his reaction, but he kept on and on about you being in danger because of me, and how the hell could I call it love, until I finally told him in no uncertain terms to shut up!'

'Oh, no!' wailed Jessica. So that was why her father was so upset! She had wondered what her parents would say if they found out about the marriage before she had a chance to explain.

'Oh, yes! Anyway, I agreed with him on one point, that I should give you room; and a chance to think without the pressures I've been subjecting you to lately.' He grinned and reached across for her hand, lifting it to his lips.

Jessica blushed, and said, 'I was miserable, Adam. I thought I'd misunderstood you, that you didn't want me.'

He raked her with a glance. 'Don't ever think that again,' he said roughly as he turned into the driveway. 'I'll always want you.'

Such a short distance, thought Jessica looking at the house—barely four blocks. She remembered the first day when she had walked it, along the beach.

'But, Adam, why did you come for me tonight? What changed your mind?' she asked as they got out of the car.

Adam retrieved her bags and led her up the steps to the porch. He put the bags down and dug into his pocket for the key. After unlocking the door he put the bags inside and reached for her, smiling tenderly. 'This time we do it right,' he said with conviction as he lifted and carried her across the threshold. 'I love you, Jessica Gentry Oakman.' His arms tightened for a moment and he kissed her upturned lips before setting her on her feet.

'And I love you,' she murmured, her arms still locked around his neck. They moved and her foot hit something. She looked down. It was another suitcase. Her eyes flew to his. 'You were leaving!'

'For now,' he nodded. 'I was a fool. But, Jess, I couldn't think straight!' His arm was close around her, guiding her to the sofa where he sat down and pulled her on to his lap.

She turned her face to him in anticipation of his kiss, but he evaded her mouth with a groan to bury his face in her hair.

'Let's get these damned explanations out of the way, Jess. If I ever start kissing you, I'll never stop.' He lifted his head to look deeply into the violet eyes. 'I was going to give you a week to clear your mind and see if you missed me.' He kissed the tip of her nose, grinning, then he sobered. 'When I came back here tonight after you all left I knew I had to get out. I couldn't stand this house without you. I took a quick shower and crammed some things into a bag. I was going to the airport and take off—I had no idea where to, but I had to get away from here.' He paused. 'But when I took this windbreaker from the halltree and put it on there was something in the pocket.'

Jessica looked at him questioningly. It was the blue windbreaker she had worn earlier today, on the beach.

He reached in the pocket and withdrew something. It was the box she had asked Dennis to bring.

Jessica's eyes glimmered in understanding and she smiled up at him. 'Oh, Adam . . . this is why you didn't leave?'

He nodded, returning her smile.

She took the box from his hand and opened it. Her grandfather's wedding ring was wedged into a slit in the bed of black velvet. She lifted it and read the inscription aloud ' "To John 1-25-30 Love Jess." I was named for my grandmother,' she said shyly.

He was looking at the ring on her palm. 'When I saw it I must have stood for five minutes staring at it. Then I started wandering through the house. I didn't know what to do. I'd promised your father I'd leave you alone for a while.'

'Adam! Oh, darling!' she cried, feeling his pain.

'I went from room to room searching for you like a madman. And I found you, Jess.

'I went into the kitchen and there were the two steaks you'd taken out of the freezer. Two! And potatoes wrapped in foil. Two! I looked in the refrigerator and there was the salad, and the table was set for two. You'd been waiting for me, darling, and I'd sent you away. But you were still here. You filled this house with your loving and turned it into a home. Without you it's just another house.' His voice was thick and his arms tightened as he buried his face in her hair. 'God, I love you!'

Jessica wound her arms around his neck, holding him. Tears glistened in her eyes. Adam said something she couldn't hear and she pulled back slightly.

He lifted his head and looked down into her

glowing face and with a finger wiped away a tear. 'That was when I knew that if I had to go on my hands and knees to your father, I was coming for you.' He smiled grimly. 'Fortunately, Dennis had been talking for us and your father had calmed down. We have their blessing, darling—grudgingly given, but we have it. I must have looked like the wrath of God when I walked in there and told them I'd come to take you home.' He laughed hollowly. 'Because they were speechless for a minute. Then your father said "Go up and get her, son." ' Adam's hand shook slightly as he smoothed her hair back from her face. 'We'll go back tomorrow. We'll explain everything, but tonight is ours. You've been my bride, my darling, now I want you to be my wife.'

Jessica opened her fist. The gold ring lay there. Adam held out his hand and she slid it on to his finger.

'And I want to be,' she whispered softly, and then all thoughts were suspended as he began to kiss her deeply, passionately, and she responded with everything in her.

Adam stood up holding her close to his broad chest. His lips never left hers as he carried her down the hall to the bedroom.

They slept exhaustedly, like tired children, while a tiny sunbeam intruded between the curtains and crept slowly across the carpet. When it touched Jessica's eyes she wriggled in Adam's arms and hid her face against him. A deep rumbling chuckle under her ear brought her fully awake, and she twisted her head to look up into his smiling face.

For a moment they stared at each other in ecstatic remembrance of the passion they had shared during the night, then Adam groaned and pulled her on top of him. 'I love you! I never thought it was possible to love someone the way I love you,' he murmured against her cheek.

Her mouth sought his eagerly. His hands stroked her back from shoulder to hip and she trembled at his touch. Those caressing hands, his sensual mouth, and his hard body had brought her the ultimate experience of soaring pleasure.

Finally she lifted her head to look down at him through her lashes.

'Aren't you hungry?' she teased with a shaky smile.

'Starved!' he answered, rolling her on to her back. Then he was above her, seeking her parted lips. She lifted her arms to wind them around his neck, her fingers raking the black hair.

Adam raised his head just far enough to say against her mouth, 'Where did you get the painting in Mother's room?'

'In Alexandria. Do you like it?' she murmured, her desire rising under his intoxicating touch.

'Um, I guess so. Why did you buy it?' His eyes were gleaming through narrowed lids as he covered her face and throat with light tantalising kisses.

Jessica caught his face in her hands and looked at him in mock exasperation. 'You know very well why I bought it. It looked like you did that day.' She let her fingers trail down his cheek and laughed huskily as his eyes darkened. 'That wonderful day when I met you, fell in love with you and married you, all before dinner!'

He smoothed the tumbled glory of her hair and tucked it behind her ear. 'There's something else special about that day, you know,' he told her lovingly.

She frowned. 'Something else?'

He held up the hand wearing the ring she had put there. 'It was January the twenty-fifth. Your grandparents' anniversary!'

Her eyes were alight with happiness. 'That makes it perfect! Oh, Adam, I love you!' She pulled his head down to meet her lips, and there was no more conversation for quite a while.

Later Adam asked, 'Where do you want to go for a honeymoon?' His hands laced through the golden silk of her hair tumbled across his chest.

Jessica lifted her head to look at him. 'Can't we stay here?' she asked lazily, stretching like a cat warmed by the sun.

His arms tightened. 'That's what I'd like, too. We can take a trip later,' he said with satisfaction, his lips against her forehead. 'We'll have to go to

Atlanta soon, so you can meet my mother. I hope you'll like her.'

'Oh, Adam, I hope she'll like me!'

'She'll love you!' he chuckled. 'She's dropped broad hints for years that I should have a wife. She didn't know that I had to wait for you to grow up!' He dropped a kiss on her nose. 'And now, my little beachcomber, we have to beard the lion in his den. Your father is probably pacing the floor, waiting for us.'

Jessica giggled softly. 'Daddy isn't half as bad as he appears, Adam—and you'll have to admit, it must have been a shock!'

Adam fried bacon while Jessica scrambled eggs. They ate at the small table in front of the window, relishing the smallest touch, the smallest glance at each other in their new-found love.

Then they walked slowly along the beach, until her parents' home was in sight. The arm around Jessica's shoulder pulled her closer and hers, around his waist, tightened in response.

'I love you,' Adam murmured, looking down into her face.

Jessica's eyes glowed, and she reached up on tiptoe to kiss him. 'I wonder if anyone has ever been as happy as I am,' she whispered.

They were so absorbed in each other as they walked that they didn't see the other couple who waited for them. The man's arm came out to gather the woman to him. She tilted her head back to look up, smiling tenderly. He returned her smile and said with a catch in his voice, 'I haven't forgotten the feeling, have you?'

She answered, 'I hope they'll always be as happy as we are.'

Harlequin® Plus

MOUTH-WATERING CHEESECAKE

There's nothing quite like good cheesecake for dessert. When Adam takes Jessica to the Jockey Club for dinner, he tells the maitre d', "I've looked forward to bringing my wife to sample your cheesecake" – so the dessert must have been something very special. What a shame that an urgent phone call kept the pair from eating it!

Below is a recipe for mouth-watering cheesecake. Try it, serve it to family or guests, and watch them come back for more!

What you need:

- butter
- 2/3 cup almonds, finely chopped
- 2½ lb. plain cream cheese
- 3 tbsp. flour
- 1¾ cups sugar
- grated rind of 1 lemon
- 1 tsp. vanilla extract
- 5 whole eggs
- 2 egg yolks
- ¼ cup whipping cream, not whipped

What to do:

Preheat oven to 475°F. (245°C.). Butter a 9-inch springform pan. Sprinkle chopped almonds on bottom and sides of pan to form a crust. Chill while preparing filling. Using an electric mixer on low speed, blend together cheese, flour, sugar, rind and vanilla till smooth. Beat in eggs and yolks, one at a time, till thoroughly mixed. Stir in cream. Pour filling into chilled crust. Bake for 10 minutes. Lower temperature to 200°F. (95°C.) and bake for 1 hour and 15 minutes, or until a knife inserted in center comes out clean. Cool on rack, then chill, preferably overnight. Makes 12 servings.